PERSONAL STORIES

PERSONAL STORIES

JEFFREY ELLINGER

ISBN-13: 9780692758533
ISBN-10: 0692758534

To Joanne

Λ HISTORY OF EVERYTHING

First is something floating through infinity. Nowhere it is not, and nothing it cannot do.

Alone, with endless power, it decided to make everything. All luminous matter spread out like displaced water from its celestial finger in a pool the size of the universe. Many of its happiest moments are in this time: of days, years, eons. Though it knows nothing of time, even though it knows everything.

In one corner of its canvas a globe began to sprout tiny creatures. As they sprang forth, it found them adorable, each one more than the last. It loved them. Though even with being omnipotent, it could not speak to them, as it knew that would only scare them. So it stood back and watched them move and begin to speak and do things like care for the tinier adorable creatures, so small. Just specks of dust.

It watched them grow crops from the fertile soil, and that made it happy, that the little creatures would make the ground prosperous. Sometimes they offered gifts from the fertile ground. They would even sacrifice one of the other adorable creatures as an offering to it for more crops from the ground, which made it sad, that the little adorable creatures would kill so wantonly. To see one of them die so needlessly was too much. But it did not intervene. It just watched and hoped the creatures would get smarter and the smaller baby creatures would grow up and teach the next generation of baby creatures until there were hardly any more lessons they could pack into their stupid little adorable heads.

Meanwhile, events rippled the rest of everywhere. Events the little creatures could never hope to understand. Blackness ate blackness. Suns lived and died. Galaxies sped away from the center spark. When it found time, even though it did not know time, it would hold the original spark and feel the warmth of creation.

Though no matter how warm, it could hear the cries of the creatures. And though it did not want to admit this to itself, all it wanted to do was drown everything. So it did just that, letting only two of each of the creatures survive. It felt cleaner afterward, renewed. Even though it was always the same.

When everything dried up, it was glad to see the creatures picking up the pieces. But as soon as they got going, they got the terrible idea to make a building tall enough so they could talk with it, and ask questions like, "What's the deal with everything?" and "When are we going to the place in the sky so we can be happy with you?"

The questions annoyed it, since it had no answers. When the creatures died, they died, and they became soil for other creatures. It did not want to explain that. So, as the little creatures were making this giant tower, it decided to toss them in every direction, ensuring they could no longer communicate with each other. Now it would be much harder for them to come up with their harebrained ideas, like building a tower to the sky. And while it would always feel bad about doing this, what could it do? It could not drown them again. It had made a promise, and it had invented promises.

From then on, it would have to live with what it made, however messy and ugly it forever became.

Λ COMIC'S TRAGEDY

We waited for the bus. Not far away, close enough we could hear, a man dressed in a Santa suit rang a bell for charity. "Santa can stand on his own," I said. "He is an independent Claus."

Joanna did not laugh. She buried her chin in the collar of her jean jacket. It was much colder than when we started shopping. Now it was snowing lightly. I continued.

"A Weather Channel headline that reads: Weather's fine. You look great. Most likely you'll never see a sinkhole. Have a good week."

More snow fell. Cars sloshing around. A car with Georgia license plates drove by.

"Pears," I kept going with the game. "A kind of fruit. Goes right after peaches and plums." She would one day write a song using that one.

We waited for the bus in silence. The night before an acquaintance of mine, someone I'd described to Joanna as "a girl who reviewed my jokes and gave me feedback," had sent a picture of her ass, purple splotches on both cheeks, from what she called a "play party." Joanna saw it on accident. Standing in the cold, waiting for the return trip, I didn't want us to dwell. I thought about a couple of movies we'd recently seen in the theater.

"Or what about this: *Eternal Sunshine* is *Primer*, but for English majors."

Blazing Saddles, Old School, Duck Soup, basically every movie my comedy friends deemed canonical, she'd never seen, and it made her all the more attractive, but she was already attractive. Golden blonde hair and a wonderful body. She is well-known now because of her songs, and because of who she is married to, but back then I don't think she realized her looks. Here, years later, the main thing I worry about is who is going to worry about all the things that don't change when I worry about them when I die. There are no answers. Only more questions.

My stomach rotted as we waited for the bus. I didn't want to apologize again, having done that many times. I thought about crying, and I would have done it had we not been in public. She saved me by speaking for the first time in hours.

"What about," she said, her voice dry. "What if every week is the week between Christmas and New Year's and we live in peace and there is no candy corn."

"Sounds good," I said, rejuvenated. "You know what my motto is."

It was our joke. I'd say, "You know what my motto is," trail off, then say "huh" when she asked what my motto actually was. It was dumb, but she always played along. This time, she grimaced. "Or how about the motto is don't give up, or do, it doesn't matter, the sun fades and the earth grows cold and everything is forgotten." I paused, watching a car drive, leaving fresh tracks through the parking lot. "I'm not sure what that makes for an acronym."

Snow fell on Joanna's hair. I wanted her to play the game, the one where we spontaneously thought of jokes for my routines.

"From now on," Joanna began. I liked standing by her, knowing other people saw us and assumed we were together. But she didn't finish.

We met online through a website, not an app, like they do now. The website where, ten years ago, the endeavoring yearning artists met, the ones with crappy day jobs who at night toiled away in dingy bars with a microphone in front of a bad open-mic crowd, then at home in their spare time accrued calluses from a guitar or a keyboard. I knew, from the moment I saw her profile, I wanted her, but I never thought she'd respond, then she did, and we met. Later came the prolonged engagement and one miscarriage and not long after she went with another comedian. His name is Andy, and he ended up as her husband.

We fought in the mall about everything two people could fight about, and by the end we weren't talking. I hadn't bought anything. She'd gone off and called one of the friends she always called when we had our arguments as I imagined taking off her clothes. Joanna had a round backside for a harp-playing folk singer, and subtle brown moles on her face and neck. We lived in Minneapolis. I thought of a musician from the city.

"How about this," I said, shivering in the cold." Come over tonight with that purple body pillow and we'll pretend we're polyamorous with Prince."

Joanna smirked, but nothing more. She carried two bags, each of them precious in her hands. The bus came and we got on, sitting next to each other but not speaking. Above the windows were lawyers advertising their services for worker's comp claims. After about fifteen minutes, I couldn't take it anymore. Joanna had been wiping away tears.

"It would probably bum out a lot of writers if they knew that the only people jealous of writers are other writers." But Joanna said nothing. The bus took us home.

I went to the kitchen and she went to the bedroom. In the refrigerator, the last of our almond milk. Joanna was the only one who ever drank the stuff, and since a habitual loop ran in my head to come up with a joke or an astute observation about whatever was in front of me, I said to myself, "If you've never had almond milk, that's probably okay."

Around ten at night, I flipped through the channels with my snack. The late-night shows started their monologues, the ones I once religiously watched. I lit up my one-hitter and tried to let the day's intensity wash away. I knew she'd smell and come scold me. I heard her playing her harp mournfully. A commercial for baby formula came on, and I wrote down, "You can't spell teat without eat, says a baby."

I packed my bowl tighter and took a longer hit, sending the coughing fits through me. Very soon, I'd be thinking of all kinds of ideas. I had hair then and probably looked handsome enough that when I went to open-mic nights it didn't seem so sad. Even cynical members of the audience could have reasonably thought, "Hey, this guy is trying like everyone else. Hell, maybe he'll get there, if he catches a break."

Joanna was younger than I and already enjoyed more success. She had opened for a national act for several dates in the Midwest and released an EP and a national label had picked her up for her first album. We were near the end on that day of the mall. I didn't know it; I was high. My notepad in front of me, I came up with what I thought was the best stuff.

Always been thirty and flirty. Always will be.

"Liquid Dreams" by O-Town is in the top 5 for songs about nocturnal emissions sung by MTV-created boy bands of the early '00s

Just because you're heartbroken and God made an eternal hellfire and nothing works out the way you plan and you're alone doesn't mean you should be sad

Nothing more intimate than a serious deodorant commercial

I want to say I watch *Room Raiders* because of the butts but I know deep down I watch it hoping someone will find love in this godforsaken world

If Super Blog Man came to save me from a tall burning building I'd just take my chances on the jump

He's not even all that. At moist, he's a sponge.

If given the choice, I would take work over banging a drum for eight hours straight

All toothbrush commercials are the same. Think about it.

Someone I once liked is now dating a man who resembles a Keebler Elf. Note to self: Start cookie-making factory inside of a tree.

I look forward to falling for you as much as I look forward to writing the email asking why it didn't work out

It's weird that you could go outside right now and see an animal flying in the air, right?

A petition to boycott reincarnation, at least until it promises to give new souls a chance

I like to refer to events that happened earlier in the day as back in the day

Years later now, and I wish I could find the energy to finish this story about Joanna and me. We loved each other. Now she's gone, famous and married to a successful comedian named Andy. I've never found him that funny. I know that sounds like sour grapes. I tried to be a comedian. I brushed alongside Joanna's current husband, even. The same age as me, but already in the upper class of our improv group. We found that unfair, me and a few other hardened comics in the intermediary class, believing he shot up that fast because he knew somebody, though now with age on my side I'm sure it had more to do with several of the younger women in our class thinking he was very good-looking. Looks or favoritism or his talent or all three, it doesn't matter. Average people have to work harder, and I did, for a time, which is maybe what Joanna saw in me, that when we met I was trying. And I remember she once said I was "wonderfully sweet."

Joanna is not in my bedroom playing her harp and singing her songs. When I first met her she played an acoustic guitar like everyone else. I actually bought her her first harp. At a garage sale, the person selling it only offered the frame without the strings. Joanna thought it might be fun to try and fix it up. So I bought it for $25 and things took off from there.

Last night I got high and wrote in my notebook again. Every so often I still get the urge to go to an open–mic. I am becoming less capable of standing in front of a crowd without the crushing doubt and fear. It's probably more a condition of my age and my increasing decrease in hair and the fact that Joanna is gone, but fewer people believe in me, and when I say fewer I mean almost none. My parents never did, even in the time when I started to get paid for comedy, opening for semi-famous acts when they rolled into basement clubs around Minneapolis and St. Paul. I secretly think my parents hated that period in the early '00s the most, since it gave me hope for the future in an untenable field where I would never make it.

Taking another hit and looking at my jokes now, I don't know, maybe I could do some kind of Mike Birbiglia thing. Take the audience through a journey of excruciating bleak detail while recounting all my failures. Paint a scene of me and Joanna in a fight. Exaggerate how we used to talk to each other. She was recently in a nationally released movie directed by what critics call an auteur. Some consider him to be the best American director, and my ex-lady is starring in his movies. My hippie with the moles and the golden blonde hair and harp, she's out there now. I don't believe the audience would accept that she was once mine.

I sit here and look at my journal and think for a second that what I have written is better and smarter than what most comedians have, and there is a conspiracy holding me back. I have only a few hundred Twitter fans, and that number dwindles each day. Compare that to someone coming up now: premade with hundreds of thousands of followers out of the gate and whatever they do goes viral. It's not a matter of whether their art is redeemable, what becomes popular is a matter of what we, as a viewing audience, will tolerate. We don't seek out the best; we put up with the lowest common denominator until we put up our hands and say, "Okay, that's about enough of that, what else you got?" at which point someone gives us more garbage. Mitch Hedberg is forgotten now and Andy has one of the most popular television shows and is married to Joanna.

"There is nothing after we die. Only blackness." I could say that to an audience. They might laugh.

Joanna used to tell me, after things started to fall apart and I didn't get as many gigs and her first album was about to come out, that all the weed I smoked sucked me of my ambition. It was my hope, I told her early on, to be one of the greatest comedians of a generation.

"Doesn't matter if they don't recognize it," I said in all seriousness to her. "Someday they will."

The room has a cloud of smoke and I think, I am only thirty-six years old. That's still sorta young. James Murphy released his first album around that age. Monet was not well known until his mid-thirties. I majored in art. It took Edward Hopper until his forties to gain an audience. Rodney Dangerfield, Phyllis Diller, Marc Maron, they didn't find their way until later in life, and sometimes not until death, like Bill Hicks.

Maybe I should start a podcast. Comment on movies while getting high, with a monologue at the beginning. Oh God, that's perfect. I should be writing this down. I'll send a tweet with my new jokes and a video of work from a few years ago to Kyle Mooney and when he comes to town we will become best friends. I'll get my own half-hour special, and soon people will see me as I should be seen, a Midwestern Louis CK, someone who toiled in obscurity for years but was a genius the whole time. The world works that way, slowly. Joanna might see me on television, late at night in her mansion where Charlie Chaplin once lived, and be overtaken with grief.

"I should have stuck with him," she'll think, looking over at her husband who will literally be playing with his own poop. "He helped me when I was low. When I was just an unknown girl with an acoustic guitar."

Before all that, I need to smoke. The rest of my life could be a wild ride. Sit and enjoy these last few seconds of anonymous relaxation.

TWO OLD DOLLS

"Wherever I go, you go." Bud repeated it, "Wherever I go, you go."

Kitty let the words drift by, staring up at the ceiling. She was always like that, or lying facedown—unless someone sat her in a chair or propped her up against pillows—and she thought, "It's not your words, Bud, but the way you say them, like they were written for you."

They met in the basement of a suburban home in the '80s. Back then, Bud adored it when Kitty tipped over for no reason. But now picturing her never-blinking eyes, Bud wanted to go back to that beginning, to when they were fresh off the assembly line and everything seemed possible.

Out of the silence Kitty said, "Everything is different now, Bud."

How pivotal, what she said, yet all Kitty could ever remember about that moment later on was how the right strap of her pink overalls dug into her shoulder, chafing her.

Bud said nothing, or maybe he just didn't hear. It's true he had a head of "soft fluff," as Kitty once called it, but like he told his beloved Kitty—or any other doll who'd listen—he used what he had as well as any best buddy.

Peering out at the desert, forehead against the window, Bud couldn't find a good place to start. Theirs was a cancerous mass, not a single strand easily pulled out. If someone pressed, Bud would have said they were in that dingy hotel room because of a silent protest. In the last months ("has it been years?" Bud thought right then) Kitty straightened her blonde hair, never braiding it, and it reminded them both—though neither spoke it—of the kind of doll they had agreed to never become. It was how a Barbie would fix her hair. How a Ken would want it.

Neither moved.

The bed, for Kitty. By the window, for Bud. They imagined the other. Bud saw Kitty's pink ribbons while Kitty could almost feel her love's straight brown hair. Still no grays emerged from below his iconic red baseball cap.

Head against the window, Bud couldn't remember how it started. Kitty was built like a softball player, healthy and strong, while the new doll boasted the kind of figure drawn from a lust-filled designer's heart. Looking out at the miles of dry heat, Bud felt his stomach drop, poring over the sordid memories of many nights discovering another's fresh stuffing.

Stillness in the abandoned hotel room. A half-empty bottle of *Teacher's* on the bureau. Neither Bud nor Kitty took a drink. Kitty, after so long, spoke. And Bud would always remember, when playing back that afternoon, how she sounded like a eulogist.

"You asked if I remember, Bud. How could I forget? I don't know if you can love someone before you know them, but that's how it was, like I was made in a factory to fit you. I've never told you, but do you remember the time when we went to that lake? In Minnesota, you and me and that young family? They laid us out beside them on that red-and-white-patterned blanket, and the two little girls kept giving us more food to eat from their picnic. The parents scolded them because we couldn't keep up, but how could we complain? It was sunny, and the lake's surface was sparkling, and you were so handsome. I never told you this, but it was that afternoon when I knew I'd always be with you. I saw your dimples and those freckles, and I thought, they are perfect because they are mine. I will always love them. But now I think about it, and that family must be gone. The mom and the dad could be retired, or even passed away. And those sweet children who smeared strawberries on our faces and poured juice down our clothes must have growing families of their own, with little ones who don't play with dolls but computer screens and video games. That beach could be overgrown with weeds. Maybe no one has come to it in years. And look at us, Bud, we can't find the energy to even leave the spots we've been in for the last, what has it been, years? Bud, you were the love of my life and you've had someone else. Jesus, I am falling apart."

Bud stayed with his soft forehead against the window. He wanted to reach for a glass of the whiskey, but a drink would only prolong the inevitable. He'd have to be sober for this, so instead he tried to think of how he could get to the plastic keys sitting beside the bottle, and how, if he ever did find a way to move, he would use those keys to start a child's three-wheeler parked in rocks near a deserted outdoor pool he and Kitty would never float on top of, and eventually sink.

ROOMMATES

They had been roommates for a year at the faltering edge of their twenties. One lived upstairs and called himself a writer. The other, the owner of the house, lived on the main floor and woke up each weekday morning for a good job as an elementary schoolteacher. Years earlier they met at an evangelical summer camp. Two balding college students from the Midwest who suspected early on they would stay in touch for the foreseeable, and unforeseeable, future.

Neither possessed a steady Christian girlfriend then, and they bonded over that, discussing what it meant to be single under the Lord, studying passages in the New and weighing them against what was said in the Old. Both the writer and the schoolteacher held doubts concerning the literal meaning of the scriptures, but neither spoke them. They carried their consternation like an invisible yoke, especially so the writer, who appeared weak standing next to those who kept their visors backward, their sandals open-toed, and their arms upraised while leading the rowdy, hour-long praise and worship sessions.

Contrasted against those larger and often hairy men, bound for jobs in leadership, it's no wonder neither the schoolteacher, who was serious and smart, nor the writer, who was sensitive and hopeful, found a wife that summer. They found Jerry instead, a man in a frock who traveled with a band of ascetic nomads, all in similar homemade attire. Jerry had a beard down to his waist and preached under the hot Texas sun all day, every day. So magnetic was his personality that after the summer ended, the schoolteacher sold all of his possessions—which were meager like the woman in the Gospel of Mark who gave up everything—and followed Jerry. But not even the winter hit before the schoolteacher—who'd sold his things, bought a van, and visited a fair amount of college campuses throughout the Midwest—gave up on Jerry, as well as Jesus, and moved in with a woman.

For years, the writer did not give up on God. Not until after a failed relationship, at the end of a series of failed relationships, did he come to the realization that it was not the purity of his prayers, but the density of his luck, the tenacity of his determination, the attractiveness of his face, that would land a wife. When the writer stumbled upon that objective truth, the earth did not swallow him up, as he once feared it would. No, he found himself in a place where red wine seemed to flow down the mountains and straight into the mouths of unattached women. That is, he had moved from his one-room apartment in Sioux Falls to a shared house in Seattle, where he began work for a package delivery company, and as he started to slide away from faith, the writer trekked beyond the restrictions of youth, to the places where he and those he met could become, as the writer once read in the scriptures, "one flesh." The writer lost his virginity, and for a time he lived in happiness.

As another earth unfurled in the Pacific Northwest, the schoolteacher settled in a part of Minneapolis with "the good bars and restaurants," as a band from the suburbs of Edina once sang. The writer visited the schoolteacher in that time and found Minneapolis to be a fine place to meet prospects for a wife. She was what the writer still wanted, Christian or not. The schoolteacher, on the other hand, did not talk openly of personal things. Discussing matters of his heart was like prying open a clam without a knife. All the writer knew, really, was that his old friend had turned into a Don Juan after reading a book called *The Finesse*. But using tricks and games and illusions of status to find the love of your life seemed cardinally wrong to the writer, who believed love could not be engineered. The schoolteacher was more pragmatic and found long-term girlfriends by putting on eyeliner, giving out a fake name, and pretending he was not interested in breasts, even though they were what he adored, almost more than anything.

The two old friends went about their lives, the writer in Seattle futilely trying to make his way as a novelist, while the schoolteacher plugged along with a girlfriend, who changed names every year or so, and at his job, where he was a rock star, bringing his guitar to class—the same one that once played chords for Christ—and conducting sing-alongs with his students. They laughed and learned and the schoolteacher continued up the ladder, aging into his thirties. That's around the time he decided to enter the next stage of adulthood, finding a one-story, post–World War II model home in the first suburb of the city, Richfield, a neighborhood with '50s-era bowling lanes and a store just for the buying and fixing of typewriters. His timing, though, was not good. The schoolteacher bought in right before the banks fell and mortgages turned upside down, so he was very glad—the schoolteacher almost found himself not so mockingly thanking God—when his old friend, the writer, called to say he would be moving back to the Midwest.

Along came a woman to make them a trio. While working at a bike store in the Ballard neighborhood of Seattle, she came to understand that even if she enjoyed an artist's lifestyle, she could not for the rest of her life have casual sex with bike boys in a band or parkour enthusiasts who had some paintings in a gallery, so she applied to law school in her native Minneapolis and was accepted. But just before she went off to school, fate intervened, and the law student met the writer. Online, as people do, and their first date went so well it ended in bed. Soon after, and not because the writer wanted to, they lost touch. Not until he moved to Minneapolis did he find her again by accident.

The writer had gone back online searching, even if he would say, sometimes mournfully to those dim enough to ask, that his "best

chances were behind him": Megan, Katherine, Anne, names disap-
peared and maybe even married. Still he searched for Her, whoever
she was, and he happened to find the law student. On a computer
screen in the attic of the schoolteacher's house, there she was: light
brown hair, wholesomely plump, never one to be picked first at
junior high dances but good-looking in a way the writer would
always desire. Her screen name was LightTrouble, and where it
asked what others first noticed, she answered straightforwardly,
"Coming from the front, my smile, from the back, my butt. That's
just how it is."

But it was not the shape of the law student's behind or the sym-
metry of her lips that most accurately told her story, instead, how
she answered the question, so directly. The writer would always
remember that night in Seattle after they ate pho at a Vietnamese
restaurant, he parked the car on the street by her rented house and
they began to kiss. When it got too heated, the law student pulled
away and asked, "You wanna just come inside?"

He loved that. The writer emailed the law student in Minneapolis
hoping she had not changed, and they agreed to see each other
once more. They met at a bar where the law student came in wearing a black cotton dress—close around her hips, clinging to her
breasts—along with a jean jacket to partly hide her curves. She was
pretty, the writer thought, even if the schoolteacher said nothing
about her in the car on the way home. Undeniably, she brought a
brightness. While they drank beers and ate burgers and fries they
talked about the cities they had lived in, what they had done, how

they got to be what they were. Of the three, the law student most wanted to meet up again. And they did, in a way.

Days later, the smell of breakfast wafted upstairs to the writer. The night before he'd heard a woman's voice, brief and fleeting, though not until he came downstairs that morning—political talk show on the TV in the living room—did he see a fussy mess of familiar hair, a jean jacket on the couch, and the law student's hands massaging the top of the schoolteacher's bald, white head.

"Hey Johnny," the schoolteacher said. Johnny was the schoolteacher's nickname for everyone, not the writer's real name.

"Good morning," the writer said, scratching his own bald head.

"Good morning," the law student said without turning.

Shocked, the writer went to the kitchen for juice and right back upstairs to bed.

It was disheartening, and yet the writer was glad whenever the law student would come over and the three would drink out of an aluminum bowl filled with alcohol and fruit juice and after they became tuned enough the schoolteacher would bring out his guitar and they would sing until passing out at some hour of the morning. It was the kind of fun people too old for dancing at clubs downtown could have. For months it went that way, until the day the schoolteacher came home after dining out at a restaurant which had, according to him, "the best happy hour in town," though the writer would never be convinced. It seemed to him overpriced, the kind of place where women wore animal-skin jackets with leopard-print shirts and men wore pointed shoes and dark jeans. As the schoolteacher washed dishes, an unnatural restlessness hung in the air. Normally the schoolteacher would be on the couch, laptop on his lap, the television on. That evening, he just blurted it right out.

"So we were eating, and she asks, 'What are we doing?' then she says something about us 'going out.' So I said, I didn't think we were going out, I thought we were 'hanging out.' And then she started crying and it was a whole thing. But what the fuck, right?"

"Yeah," the writer said, pretending to sympathize. "What the fuck." Though all he could think about was the schoolteacher breaking up with the law student, and her freckled breasts and large backside never being touched by his philistine hands ever again.

The next weekend in the living room, the television on in the background, the schoolteacher in bed, the law student sloppily told the writer, between tears, what once transpired between her and a previous boyfriend who recently got engaged to a "beautiful Indian woman." The writer listened and thought what the law student's tears were really for the schoolteacher, but he did not press. The law student and the writer had started to kiss, right there on the couch.

The law student slept in the schoolteacher's bed that night, but in the morning she came upstairs to the attic, as she did in the coming months. The writer never asked why. Those wonderings evaporated as she slid, naked and cool, under his sheets. He was thankful to live in a world where she spent the sober, intimate morning hours with him. The routine became evenings with the schoolteacher, mornings with the writer. She'd get ready to leave after the schoolteacher left and a few hours before the writer went to his, in his words, "bullshit factory job." In the writer's attic, the writer would admire the law student's form as she put on her underwear, hardly covering her, then watch her get bundled up—as it was a cold time of year—and adamantly tell her to stay in the bed. Sometimes, she listened, but usually he walked her downstairs, no matter how much she protested. In the evenings after work the writer acted the same, as a roommate living his life, while the schoolteacher worked on his side business making apps. Both watched late-night sports recaps, their usual brief conversations highlighted with an occasional reference to the law student. Even the writer brought her up, if only to keep up appearances.

One particularly drunken Saturday night after coming home from the city, all three opened bottles of wine and had a fine night. The next morning, the schoolteacher went to work to decorate his classroom for the spring session—turning winter whites on corkboards into green grasses and flowers—as the law student padded up the stairs and curled into the writer's arms. No questions asked and the writer lay there after, lost in warm feelings, as he watched the law student's body rise and fall. With all those good sensations coursing in his veins, there was no way he could have stopped to think of the schoolteacher turning his car around, nor did the writer notice, as he was drowning in too much relaxed pleasure, the first turning of the front-door knob. He did perk up when the her body jerked off his.

Sitting up, the writer tried to meet the law student's eyes, but she just stared ahead as the sounds started softly below them. Louder and quicker with more intent, to the basement, and back to the main floor. Doors opening, closing. Then, everything stopped, and that must have been, the writer thought later, when the schoolteacher decided whether or not he should knock, whether an invasion of privacy was worth it or whether a roommate, a friend, a brother— back when they believed they lived forever with God—should be kept around for the rent money.

Footsteps across the kitchen. A hard closing of the front door. A car reversing out of the driveway.

The schoolteacher drove away, and the two upstairs fell back on the bed. The writer draped his arm over the law student. She pushed it off, and they lay there not touching one another. Minutes went by. The sound of lazy traffic in the suburbs. Birdsong in a nearby tree. Planets turned as heavy as stones.

THE GALAXY EXPLODES WHEN YOU MEET SOMEONE NEW

Awake. Arise. Your round earth turns. Far away, monkeys in the jungle swing from branch to branch. Elephants on the savannah lift their trunks to the sky. Bears in the mountains roar. A commotion carries to your bed, and pulls open your crusted eyes.

Her chest fills with air. Her shoulders gently drop. How sweet is this light breathing. You inch the blanket onto her. She sleeps as you stand before your bedroom mirror. Majestically, like the peoples of the tundra who stand before their igloos with fresh morning kills of pink salmon and blubbery whale.

Now they lay down their gifts. The heavens breathe in an anxious inhale.

She rustles, and you freeze. You are the statue David, your manhood dangling as the worms emerge from the ground, dancing their worm dances. She flips her body and buries her head in your pillow. Now you can move again, but for a moment you admire her. You've already planned your future together.

Put on pants and go to the kitchen like a king of a savage but grand world where everyone in the royal court eats massive legs of hearty meat. Turn on the burner.

Warmth shoots out, as it does from the beacon fires now being lit in every nation. Make your eggs. Your toast and your coffee. Everything prepared, set on your humble kitchen table. A choir sings as she emerges. The villagers in ancient lands emerge from their tents to spread out centerpieces of flowers, tablecloths of fine linens, feasts of breads and fresh fruits, creamy milks and aged cheeses. This is a day of celebration.

Your sweatshirt is soft and gray, and it must have been touched by the hand of God, because she is pulling you close and kissing you. An angel kisses you, from the heavens now pregnant with songs of hosanna. Like a servant, you hand her breakfast, and she receives it like holy communion.

"So good," she says, smiling a toothy smile. The earth could not contain it. The entire galaxy could barely be its boundary.

"I'm cold," she says as she eats. She is Christ, dying for your sins on Golgotha. She can save you from the flames of hell. "Can I borrow your sweatshirt?"

"Sure," you say. "Yes, of course."

Stars explode, new planets form. The lightest of elements, the heaviest of dark matter. Breakfast occurs over infinity. She has eaten. You have broken bread and she is ready to leave. She has to "meet a friend."

At your doorstep you are a hairy ape from the beginning of man. As you hug goodbye, she transfers every particle of meaning ever conjured from the consciousness of all ancestors.

Now it's over. She pats your chest and walks to her car. Growing smaller, drifting like an ocean tide. You find you are suffocating with fondness. Your only oxygen is knowing you will see her again. Your sweatshirt too.

How loud, that belief, so loud it drowns out every other voice in the world. All the world toasting to her finding someone else, someone new.

FOR NANCY, A LONG TIME AGO

Watching television in the middle of the day has always felt like a gross act. Not in the sense of what I'm watching being profane or lewd. I don't have the Spice Channel. Though it is worth quickly retelling the story of one of my classmates in high school, Jim Shartz. Jim, along with most of the guys in my class—those who started lifting in the seventh grade and drinking around the tenth grade on gravel roads or at abandoned farmhouses in the country—would go out to Jim's parents' house every Monday night and watch Monday Night Football featuring Al and Frank and Dan and, from what I understand through secondhand accounts, put on gloves and box each other like some Hemingway novel, and after that was done they'd sit around and watch the Spice Channel. These guys in my class, and the class above who would all go on to win the state championship in football two years in a row and once in track and basketball too, watched soft-core porn while the rest of the Shartz family, a mom, a dad, and a sister, sat upstairs watching *Friends* or *Seinfeld* or maybe *Will and Grace*, though I doubt the last. I grew up in an agrarian community that was very conservative.

Who knows. Maybe my classmates watching soft-core porn isn't all that crazy. Maybe that kind of thing happens all the time. This is just a long way of getting to what I said at the beginning, about watching television in the middle of the day. What I mean is how wasteful it feels. Watching television at night after you've had a long day of work always seems earned. Downright necessary, at times. But during the middle of the day, watching even a film on AMC---Altman's *3 Women* was on the other day---you get the creeping sensation, like a dull nagging tug on your conscious, you are wasting your life, and you know the act of staring at the flashing images while light is left in the day is eating your brain.

Since I currently have no job or prospects, I've been watching a lot of television lately, like yesterday, and probably later again. Prone on my couch, the right side of my face in the cushion with the left side lifted enough to make it possible to see the big screen comfortably, I watch *Cops*. It's the only show for me. My ex liked *The Real Housewives*, and I didn't have a problem with that. I didn't see it as a harbinger of doom. A lot of people, if given the choice, would participate in a reality show for the simple reason that they already have a lot of money.

Getting subjective. Here are the facts. Watching television, one arm dangling down to the floor, the other situated so my hand grasped the top of the couch, *Cops* on, and I forgot for a second who I am or what I am doing, until the commercials start—my demographic is always bailing people out of jail or needing money through loans at exorbitantly high rates of interest—and the feeling of wasting my life comes back so strong I get a numbness in my brain like I have eaten too much candy. Problem is, nothing can take me away from this. I'm laid off from the steelyard.

The best thing I can say about life at a steelyard is at least while you're there you never have to worry about watching television in the middle of the day. The worst thing I can say about life at a steelyard is that I would not wish it on anyone, at least not life at my steelyard. Everyone at mine was either beaten down or taking shaky steps that would later make them look back and wonder why they didn't do more at the start so they didn't feel so beaten down.

I spent my first days at the shears. Fernando taught me. I liked that guy. It was the casual way about him, I think. Even while unloading thousands of pounds with a forklift, then cutting the same steel on a shear—sometimes a half inch thick—with a blade that could chop a human in half, life drifted by Fernando, as if he were back in his home country of Ecuador drinking a guava drink out of a straw. Eventually, he got fired, as did Eduardo and Franklin and the other Ecuadorians, along with a bunch of white guys with the same name. I know all white people don't have the same name. It's just, at this steelyard, many did.

They all got fired for different reasons, though. Either they didn't show up on time, or they filmed themselves at their workstation like teenagers taking selfies, or, in the case of Rob—possibly his name was Mike or Tim—they dropped a full pallet of 22-gauge #4 stainless steel while attempting to place the pallet on a table for a shear job, and because 22-gauge #4 stainless steel is so thin, the edges like razors, and expensive, the whole pallet worth close to $10,000, you realize, like Rob-Mike-Tim, the steelyard bosses are going to fire you, or at the very least make you take a urinalysis, so you also know, if you are Rob-Mike-Tim and just about everyone who ever worked with Rob-Mike-Tim, that you are not going to pass a urinalysis. so you walk out the door and never come back.

I took over the shear after Fernando got fired, and from time to time I went over and bent steel at the brake press. Though really that meant I assisted the guys who did the work. Edwin was in charge, and he tried to teach me. For a time, I was supposed to learn. The ones in charge wanted great things for me. Problem was, I could never understand Edwin. Even though he was a nice guy and he knew his stuff, we couldn't communicate. But even if Edwin's English had been perfect, it wouldn't have mattered. I wouldn't have been able to run a brake press. To be given a blueprint and then visualize a steel part from a sheet of paper and transform that part into what it should be in real life? No, I can only dream of what my own life would be like, if it were perfect.

I am married, though we do not have a rigid arrangement; I am free to see others who are young, as my wife and I grow older. But do not mistake me for a sexist. My wife is free to see other men. Though of course she never does in this dream scenario, as she is too in love. She clings to my pant legs, dries her eyes with their cuffs when I leave in the morning, and in the evening when I return to our farmhouse she has my drink ready, along with a rare slab of meat on a plate handed over by our Korean maid. We have a dog who hardly ever barks, and I work as a professor, though my day job only takes me about a day or two a week and the rest of the time I make my rare furniture. Whenever we want, my wife and I go on trips to beaches in secluded areas of the world or parties in the city. She is highly regarded in her profession as a social media blogger, but she doesn't have to work either, so we invite people out to our farm with its grand views, and there is a pool and campfires and loud talk about important things until the sun comes up, and many partners are flip-flopped. We all love it.

I imagine that much easier than I could ever imagine how to transpose unbent steel into a usable part by reading a set of lines and numbers on a sheet.

So, since I contained no acuity for the math or the programming knowledge required to move up, I was given a job in quality control, and told, without further delay, that I would be part of management. They graced me with a meeting up in my supervisor's office. His bosses, the founder/owners—a zombie of a man and his wife with caked pink rouge on her pallid, pockmarked face who always left a trail of too-sweet perfume behind her when she and her zombie toured the grimy warehouse—were there. A man in his early forties, my immediate supervisor had worked for the company since he turned eighteen and wore a black leather jacket with red stripes on the sleeves. They all gave me encouraging smiles as they went through the homemade regulations, composed in Word and copied on paper in black and white.

As the sole member of the quality control team I was given a refurbished electric cart with a sign cut on the CNC routing machine that said, "QUALITY CONTROL." They even provided a new set of tools—micrometer and tape measure and a T square—all of which I packed in a fresh toolbox, welded to the back of my electric cart hardly large enough for one person to sit in. I then drove around the steelyard reading blueprints and orders, ensuring that those with an actual job made the right amount of parts at the right size and angle and bend. These people had worked at the steelyard for years, and I'd been there two months. As one might imagine, my new role didn't go over well.

I did not receive a raise, but even without receiving extra money I did not deserve the job. It was the easiest one in the entire place, the one normally given to the guy who'd been there the longest, and I didn't know the first thing about steel. Everyone else seemed very aware of these facts, and sooner or later I failed, since everyone in the yard made it impossible for me to be the new guy in the comically small electric cart.

Without much fanfare, my leather jacket–wearing supervisor eased me back to the shears. He referred to my demotion as "learning more about the company," though as time went by he and his bosses, Miss Piggy and Zombie Man—who actually whined when he spoke—checked up on me less, and there were no more meetings about how they saw "big things for me in the future," and I became sure that I would no longer be the next manager, of what or where, I would never know. I faded into obscurity.

Finally, after being hired and originally told I would be an estimator in the office across the street—I presume they offered me that because I graduated from college and they never received applicants who graduated from college—and after being moved from the shears to the brake press to the CNC machines to the machinist's area, where I loaded and unloaded parts, to the DOM tubes and scheduled pipes, then to the quality control job, and all the while still under the assumption I would one day have the estimator job, it was nice to be locked in at one spot. I could wake up each morning and know what I was getting into. I was not Their Guy, and everyone came to terms with that and let me be. Working at the shears, I knew, was the most straightforward job at the steelyard. I worked alone and listened to sports radio and had the day to think for myself. It didn't even sting when my leather jacket–wearing supervisor brought around a middle-aged bald man and introduced him as "Pete, the new estimator." I shook Pete's hand, knowing I wouldn't have been any good at the job anyway.

Then it happened. Miss Piggy and whiny Frankenstein sired five daughters who each successively looked like a hipper version of their mom, all wearing the black-rimmed glasses Asian women in advertising wear, the ones Buddy Holly wore. Miss Piggy started wearing them a few months after her daughters did, and by the way she walked around so proudly, you could tell they made her think she looked young again. Sadly, they made her seem desperate. All the daughters worked in the office except one. Even the two still in college popped by in the summer when they felt like it. The one I started my affair with was the largest of the five. She laughed easier than the others, and she is the one who worked in the steelyard.

On my first day when I wandered to her side of the building with the machinists and welders to find a bathroom, she seemed to be the girl from high school who I would have never considered, simply because of her size, the kind of girl the guys who watched the Spice Channel would have chided me for, calling me a "chubby-chaser." What did I care, though, as an adult? Those cavemen were long gone. Nancy, big in every aspect, had a good face, with or without the layers of makeup she wore. Unlike her sisters, Nancy projected an agreeable demeanor, like a Lutheran mom in Eden Prairie, all ready to please, lusty and full of life.

"Right down there, Jeffrey," she said as she motioned toward the bathrooms. No one at the steelyard had called me by my name, and I remember when I looked back I saw her walking away while checking me out. I know it sounds like the beginning of a cheesy half hour show my classmates in high school would have watched, but that was our start.

Still it took a while, months of flirting, until one day we happened to end up at the same bar after work. I ordered her a drink and she came back to my place, and from there we started to fuck at work. Meeting in secret areas, behind doors that needed a key, in some underground room or lockable closet no other steelyard worker would think twice about if they passed. When we got more brazen, we met in the back where they kept the overstock sheets of steel. Many times I'd walk up to her, wherever she texted me to meet, and I'd already be taking off my jeans and she'd act all shocked, her face turning red, but once secured behind a door she would take me in her mouth and finish me off quickly. Other times I'd lie back on the steel, covered in cardboard, and she'd sit on my face and I'd have her for lunch. Nancy brought condoms on occasion and she'd get on her knees and we'd do it that way, so I didn't get her dirty. Watching her pendulous breasts wobble in perfect circles with each push was sublime. Usually we were as quiet as we could be, but the steelyard's noise gave leeway. I loved to do my best to make her call out, to the point where several times, in the hush afterward, she'd get mad at me in a playful way, slapping or pinching my butt.

We saw each other little after work. I didn't watch football or know enough about cars. I wasn't even from Minnesota, so her family would not have accepted me. Also, full disclosure, there was the issue of her boyfriend. Suffice to say, the reason I am on my couch watching television during the middle of the day, wasting whatever small portion of possibility I have left, is because one day, after Nancy and I finished, we walked out from the closet where we had stuffed ourselves and into the stern faces of her mom and dad—Miss

Piggy and Zombie Husband—as well as my leather jacket–wearing supervisor. That last part seemed a cruel touch from her parents, who never seemed to approve of anything this particular daughter of theirs did. Nancy was taken one way and I was taken to the office, given my last check, and escorted out of the building.

What they thought I was going to do, I have no idea. I was too dazed to put up any fight. Even if I had been more cognizant of what was happening, if I had been as sharp as a thin piece of cut aluminum, I wouldn't have harbored any aggression toward them or been able to conjure up a sufficient argument for why I shouldn't be fired. I got in my car and went home. The sun was shining. It was very cold.

Months later, I don't have a job and am alone, and that all makes sense. I can't imagine dating an unemployed man who watches television during the day. Sometimes, though, while I'm watching and the commercials are on, or when the actual program is on it doesn't really matter, I'll zone out and wonder how Nancy's parents found out about us. It must have been I wasn't that sneaky when I told the one or two other steelyard workers I talked to that I was just eating lunch in my car. Somebody must have wanted Nancy more than I, and it was more than likely my leather jacket–wearing boss. He always slicked back his hair like Fonzie and went to the office to flirt with the girls in human resources, whether they had husbands or not.

Thinking about my past and worrying about my future. It's been almost three months and money is getting low. I need a job, though

I loathe thinking of the process. Putting a resume together makes me ill. I'd rather erode to nothing on this couch than think about what I have done so far in this life. I hate that I will always need a job. It's a shame I can't just live by a pond in a cabin up by Ely, in the Boundary Waters. Plant a garden and have a chunky wife. I imagine our lazy, hedonistic days, and Nancy, never with any clothes.

THE PASSION OF A BANANA RUNT

I'm just a banana-flavored candy. Dextrose, maltodextrin, calcium stearate, my chemistry is simple. Look how I shine from carnauba wax. My taste comes from corn syrup. Artificial flavors add a dimension, I think, but I am not a cannibal.

These are my colors: yellow 5, yellow 5 lake, yellow 6. The facts are on the box. How long I have been this way, I could not say. Time erodes like sugar.

Around me at the start, I remember the sounds of a million plinking dots falling from tumblers through the grates where the least of us got weeded out and tossed into the great white nothing. Funneled onto a conveyor, I rode alone for what seemed like miles as I glistened and cooled from the oven. After being put in the original mold, we jostled for our positions in the goo. Surrounded by the terrible heat contorting our insides, we worked into shapes. I heard the screams of those I did not know, clawing and scratching.

Without aspirations: that must have been how I was born. A confused stupid idiot. I wish I could have sensed, from out of the heavy folds of glucose, that I was supposed to move in a way that would encourage The Worker to put me down the correct path. Like anyone, I wanted to taste and look the right way, but I was blissfully unaware of the hierarchy. The words "ignorant" and "innocent" were merely concepts.

In the moments after, as we fell into our home—settling in beside other colors and flavors—I felt everything change. As they piled on top, pushing me and my kin against the cardboard walls, it fully weighed on my soul: others will have easier and brighter futures.

I let myself sink to the bottom, while the rest moved to the top. They eagerly waited to be the first out.

At the store we were purchased by a young boy, and on the car ride home he opened the box. The air felt refreshing, curling its way to where I stayed at the bottom, between other bananas and an orange. The orange's outer coat had chipped, giving him a shape like The Worker pinched him before he could fully cool. He could only talk to me out of the side of his mouth, and he was my best friend. I cried for what seems like a year to me after he left.

Only a few of us remain now. Two other bananas. One killed himself, though his body does not rot. The other is mute. Some days I try to talk to her, and every once in a while I think she's listening, but it's a trick the light plays. Inexplicably, there's a strawberry here too. She spends her days yelling to no one about conspiracies, that outside the box is heaven. I try not to listen, though some days it is nice to be reminded of a place of eternal happiness, even it is a fantasy.

I spend most of my days thinking of the beginning, of my first moments before the chaos. Warm and surrounded by family, no one seemed unhappy. We were all equal, the same gross slime, each one of us with the same uncertain chance.

SOLILOQUY OF AN ONLINE DATER

And yes those Minnesotan girls their thick sturdy legs and golden Norwegian hair but mine not so hearty we messaged each other pink circles and hers like manna from red-painted fingernails cracked skin pumped lotion from Target red circles 'round red circles those khaki pants I could tell from the start would be her words and not any other so we met at a bar under an overhanging neon sign that said Mayslack's and she came in unraveling and I stood up and we hugged and I breathed her in like clean laundry and light perfume when she smiled she was happy all youth and dark hair filling up the place like waves of black fire we floated past other dates so Midwestern tapping feet to Prince discussing followers engage and Red Wings new with novels published next year perhaps another year after that with reviews Paper Darts and Revolver yes how we sat down and caught eyes and yes this artful East Coast to Carleton girl with a grandfather who owned a block downtown the one of Gay '90s and yes that is why Minneapolis so Connecticut could wait how taken like always always falling in love from the start but this was different she had dimples like rosebuds and her eyes like chestnuts nature all exploding the universe embracing us making the bar warm and lovely and yes tonic bubbles traveling up her straw messengers of effervescence to the brain for kisses for me and only me not a fisherman or a lawyer nor a wrestler so strong because with my muscles like tree branches a force to be reckoned oh those Carleton girls their small breasts and large backsides she said to look before a trip to the ladies and when she got back she said to feel but only for a second and how the world opened and took me to heaven and Jesus sat me down and said you are special I love you look what I have showed you then the waitress came all tattoos a Vikings jersey yes Christian Ponder number 7 and asked if we wanted another and yes Alana said yes I will and so I had another too and we held hands across the table making a wicker basket carrying our emotions I paid when next we walked out interlocking so sophisticated like Manhattanites her using my wall to dampen the winds such storms but we are almost there my seat warmers friends to buns then how I said I have wanted to do this all night and hardly a moment before we kissed and after in front of her brother's house giggles between adorable she said the others all told her but I did not say if it was or was not in the back seat the heat at full blast her body pale and long near the end she said yes you are so big I think that is what she said and the glow afterward such calm serenity like husband and wife after many years I imagined yes please God if you are up there please let this be as she and I out in the cold kissing against the house yes we walked away not looking ahead but behind at each other and at home texted when she asked what would you do if you were here and I said all the things yes all the things I would do and then finally we fell asleep talking and in the morning the phone on my pillow like a mint of possibilities for all things toward good in the end then another date with karaoke "Killing Me Softly" and "River Runs Dry" and when I took her home in a cab she argued with the cab driver because she knew what it was like to be away from home she had been in Thailand her senior year and the driver was from Somalia and so I kissed her to make her quiet her facing the back seat like wild and at my place we did everything in the dark but in the light of the morning and the rest of the mornings we would explore until we knew the other better than we knew our own bodies when the next morning she called her friend on a light-filled cold Sunday and she told her she never gave that kind of affection on the first dates she was a lady and yes she was a lady a perfect lady how I then took her back to her brother's place she all bundled with a stocking hat and detachable gloves where I said goodbye and yes she would see the wrestler but how could I have known that would be the last time I would see her before she went to him the wrestler or maybe a fisherman he and his dog and her dog play in the snow of the frozen Minneapolis but later in the silence I asked and asked and yes I said you are cavalier with love, aren't you, and yes she said he has a frickin family farm near Northfield oh those Carleton girls their dimples like rosebuds their eyes chestnuts online with everyone else all dying our hearts like ash.

WORK FOR THE COMPANY

Only a few would remember the beginning, when it was just a few people and Bruce, the owner/founder of a company producing generic pharmaceuticals that would one day be publicly traded on the stock market. They worked out of a small warehouse in south Minneapolis then, and through the years the stories of Bruce—who recently sold to a conglomerate for hundreds of millions—grew. For instance, at the ten-year anniversary party in the early 1990s, when no one could figure out how to give away the floral centerpieces, and Bruce said over the microphone, "Just give it to the fattest person at your table."

Or the time Bruce gave everyone gift cards at the Christmas party, instead of the traditional three weeks' pay bonus. Everyone had already pooled up their money for Bruce's gift, and after they gave him the check at the end he said from the same microphone, "I know where this is going. Straight to the boat. You people don't know how much money I spend on that boat. Connie'll tell you." Then he pointed to his wife, Connie, who Bruce later divorced while she lay in a hospital bed with cancer. "She's always writing checks for that boat," he added.

Or the last time everyone at the company remembered. Happened a few weeks ago, when Bruce announced his company would be merging and folding under the umbrella of a much larger company that owned pharmaceutical factories around the world, in Brooklyn and Israel and Michigan. Everyone seated in the conference room, Bruce walked up to the podium wearing a leather jacket, a paisley scarf, and tight blue jeans, his hair dyed black. A spotlight shone, cutting through the dark room.

"Good afternoon," Bruce began. "I know I haven't talked to you people in a while, but I can't stay long. Have to catch a plane to Phoenix. I'm bidding on a car. In fact, if you watch the Speed Channel tonight, you might see me. What channel is Speed, Bob?" Bruce looked down at one of the suited men in the front row. Several anxiously offered their best answers. "Forty-five? No, doesn't sound right. Well, whatever it is, I can't stay long. I appreciate everyone being here. We have some important news today, so I'll hand it over to Eric."

And just like that Bruce stepped down and walked out the way he'd come in, down the center aisle. The workers in their uniforms stared.

The meeting threatened the livelihood of the workers, but they would've all said it was a nice diversion. It sliced their evening shift in half, and so work went so much faster. Another meeting planned for the following day, and the knowledge of its coming electrified a wire of joy throughout the plant. Whispers of the agenda floated, with the older workers sounding skeptical, saying things like, "They ain't telling us nothing" to the less experienced ones.

Rumors, and rumors of rumors, leaked the promise of higher-ups from the new company showing up, but those died the next day when no new faces could be found, the one everyone had seen months before, tall folks in pinstripe suits with fine-rimmed glasses and parted hair.

The meeting would be "informational," as Danny the Liquids supervisor said. They worked for an hour before filing back to the locker rooms, throwing away their hairnets, removing their steel-toed boots with their employee numbers written in white ink on the heel, and stripping out of their lab coats with the embroidered company logo. Those most sensitive to the rules took off their blue pants and put on regular jeans. Some quickly snuck outside and smoked, a haggard ash trailing behind them as they walked back in. A couple brave folks hustled out to the parking lot to move their frozen cars closer to the building. The rest headed upstairs to enjoy a moment of peace. To watch the news and drink a bottle of soda and eat a candy bar from the vending machine that just clunked out another. They watched the television. A group of Somalis, all men, grouped by the computers in the corner. A mix of others intently waited in the partitioned conference room next to the break room.

They signed the training sheet and started to think, as they settled, that this is what it must be like for management, to sit all day and talk and not do any work. A projector pleasantly hummed, lighting the agenda on a pull-down screen.

Discussion of Merger.
Efficiency and Productivity of Lines.
Uniforms and Locker Rooms.
Overview of New Processes for Audit.
What Checked By, Verified By, and Performed By Means.
Questions.

Kim, the second-shift Solids supervisor—pills and dry powders—with a bushy mustache and protruding gut clashing with his skinny arms and legs, along with Danny, who also worked second shift, herded everyone in: formulators, packagers, line leads, support services and maintenance crew; they all responded to Kim and Danny's arm-sweeping motion.

Ambling in with pops and candy, the workers sat down and signed the training sheet and cozied in for a reprieve, with only a minority erect in their chairs, wondering, almost out loud, would the new company have a strict uniform policy? Would it want to make the drug they made on their line? Would they even have a job?

The lights dimmed and Eric, the manager of managers, walked up to speak. His body made a shadow on the screen. Arms straight out against the podium, he wore beige trousers, a white dress shirt and green tie. A mustache covered his lip, and his salt-and-pepper hair was combed back with gel. For many, the only other time they'd seen Eric had been their first day. They knew, when he spoke, it was important.

"Alright," Eric said like a frog croaks. "The training sheet is getting passed around, and everyone needs to sign it." He pointed with a laser's red dot on the projection screen. "As you can see, we have quite a few things we want to go over today, and I understand we have pizza coming, so let's get started. Now, I know the first thing on everybody's mind is the merger. So let me tell you first off I know as much as each of you do, mmmkay? I'd like to know more details on the 401(k) and flex spending and what lines will be running and info like that, but, at this point, it's just not possible, mmmkay? In past lives, when something like this happened, it's usually been around the time they've said it was going to happen, mmmkay? I know that many of you are concerned, but what I will say is this: our company is very successful. What was it we made last year, Dean, five hundred million?" Dean, a first-shift Liquids supervisor in the front row, nodded vehemently. Eric continued. "I know that the new company will want to continue that success. What a company doesn't want to do is rock the boat. It's bad business to get rid of people and benefits and things like that, mmmkay. Our new company wants to grow this business and make money. That means they'll want to keep the people they have happy. That's you guys, mmmkay. Alright, I'm going to hand it over to Doug. He's going to give us some words on production."

Eric stepped down, and all the workers who wanted to ask questions were placated for the moment. It would not be until later that day, while working on their lines, that each would realize individually, "I should've asked about..." or "If I would have only thought of..."

Doug at the podium. He had graduated from Duke, or maybe Dartmouth. None of the workers knew for sure, only that Doug was the son of someone high up at the company, a friend of Bruce's. The way Doug walked up to the podium, like a rag doll, it looked as though a rod went from the bottom of his feet to the top of his head, keeping him upright. His curly hair thinned, and it seemed as though he spent too much money on overpriced stereo equipment. He began to point with the laser at numbers on the graphs and charts, stumbling as he explained why this line was getting better while that line needed work.

"But everyone's doing great," Doug said. "Almost all the stats are trending in the right direction." Eric, from his front-row chair, turned to face everyone.

"Doug's right. Just in the last month we've been trending up. Every one of you should be proud." And Eric began to clap, so all the workers did too.

Doug stepped down and handed the laser pointer over to Dean, who started up with the cleaning audit process and everyone perked up. The cleaning audit was a source of division. The workers said the company would never give the reward money out, no matter how clean everything in their production rooms became, so "it just wasn't worth it" to try and make things tidy. Dean, a round man, like a ball bearing with eyebrows, spoke with emphasis at the end of each of his sentences, declaring presidentially that it was "your audit. Each one of you must take responsibility. Reward or not, we have to be in accordance with GMP."

Good manufacturing practices—they all knew the acronym, and while none of the workers could see behind them, Danny was in the back with his arms folded, nodding his head in agreement, just as the smell of pizza wafted into the room. Eric got up without a microphone and told the workers to, "Go ahead, get some pizza." This would be their lunch break, and to have to listen to a supervisor talk, even while eating pizza, was still technically work, but they did not voice this labor issue. The workers became too intoxicated with cheese and sauce and toppings. They loaded their paper plates high as another took the stage.

Tim, the youngest of the supervisors, with a black goatee and a thick head of black hair. His clothing emphasized his youth: a button-down shirt, dark jeans, and those tipped dress shoes that seem like they are made for clowns. He began to talk about the things the others had missed: a word about the locker rooms and the continued need to keep them clean, with bullet points about what it meant to "verify" versus what it meant to "perform." The workers ate their pizza and stared at the light in the darkness. Whatever Tim said, it was fine. They processed his words as if a man preached on concepts like love and justice, and soon it came time to get back to work. Their pizza done, so was the meeting. With little protest, other than a few repressed grumbles, the workers went downstairs to the locker rooms and got dressed, and before they knew it found themselves in the spots they always stood before their second shift.

Early for their pre-work meeting, the workers stood in the white hallway. One by the phone with the company extensions, some by the Plexiglas window, and more by the sliding metal door sealing off a production room from contamination. Everywhere was white—floors, walls, doors—so white, one could almost not distinguish up from down. The workers wore white gowns that reached to their steel-toed boots, the first sign of another color in the world. White hairnets covered their heads and beard nets covered up the men's beards—even if some joked the women should be wearing them as well. They stood waiting for the day's instructions, talking about the things they talked about in the precious minutes before assignments of the day were given.

"I couldn't find anywhere to park," one said. "I had to park across the street in the church parking lot again."

A white noise filled the hall right after he said this, unlike the rooms where they made the products, where air hoses hissed and vacuums sucked up excess product and plastic caps pinged around in a metal hopper and pneumatic presses slammed hard on the glass bottles and conveyors hummed and tape machines wrenched box after box of product out of their chutes. Another woman in the hallway, her brown hair dyed, with a heavy layer of foundation on her face that made her wrinkles crack and crease like a fracturing canyon, spoke up. She tapped her foot as she talked.

"Well they didn't say anything about the parking at the meeting. I can't believe they didn't mention the parking."

"It's so bad," another piped in. A forest of stubble canvassed his neck. He pounded the wall behind him with his fists. His nervousness, some suspected, came from the drugs he once said he was addicted to. "I saw a dude parked in two spots. Doesn't no one know how to fucking park here?"

They could do nothing about the parking. It wasn't so bad long ago, back when the company was "fun to work for," as the oldest worker told the young temps. He'd been there for almost thirty years and on his lunch break he ate out of Tupperware containers as he read large-print fiction and he despised the way the company hired now, with the "foreign temps." In truth, some of the workers were lazy and ineffectual, while others were hardworking and intelligent. It's just where all of them ended up, in that hallway. The old man leaned back against the wall, waiting on the day's assignments. Roscoe gave them. He ambled down the hallway then, his feet and knees a gnarled mess from years of standing. After coming to a halt, he licked his lips.

"Everyone here?" Roscoe asked, but everyone was there. Roscoe looked around as if someone might find them. "Anybody seen Moses and Zack?"

"They're in the locker room," one of the workers said out of obligation.

"Alright," Roscoe said, licking his lips again. "We'll wait a couple minutes."

So they waited, like they always did. On the clock with nowhere to go. After a bit, two African men jogged down the white hallway, putting on their beard nets as they came. Roscoe began.

"Everybody seen the schedule?" Roscoe asked. Some of the workers wondered if one day Roscoe would not ask and instead just give the day's assignments, since that's what everyone wanted, but that never happened. Roscoe pulled down his beard net.

"Alright, I'll just go through it." And he proceeded to give the day's schedule.

Danny stood there silently. On his first day as the Liquids second-shift supervisor a few weeks before, he came to the meeting but did not speak at all, not even giving his name. To get some introductions going, Roscoe suggested the workers give their first names and a little bit about what they did at the factory—"I'm Pete. I work in Room 3423. I package suppositories"—but still Danny just stood there, barely moving his head as they went from worker to worker.

Later, when Danny did begin to talk, he did so with a considerable lisp. On several occasions in the first weeks the oldest of the factory—the one who read hardcover large-print fiction and smelled like shaving cream and could remember the beginning with Bruce—corrected the way Danny pronounced the drugs but after a few days he gave up on helping and Danny just bulled his way through it on his own.

Everyone in their spots wearing their white gowns, having already talked about parking and been given the assignments. Now they waited for Danny, who had been in the Marines and worked for a bulletproof-glass factory in Texas. He stepped into the middle of the hallway and began to pace between the two lines of workers. Danny always chose a different worker to make direct eye contact with for every other thing he said.

"Couple things: ya'll know my expectations. First, each of ya'll need to be here on time, and if ya'll can't be here on time I expect a call at least an hour before the shift starts. Where I come from, this is common sense. Number two: need ya'll to follow the pro-cedures." Danny held up a thick stapled report and shook it as a point of emphasis as he continued. "It's these procedures we have to follow to make our products. It's simple, ya'll. If you follow these practices, they won't lead ya'll down the wrong path. Follow 'em, step, by step, by step, by step. Now, number four." Some workers shot each other queer looks. "The cleaning audit, it's for ya'll. Ya'll have to take ownership of it if you wanna win the award. Every night, make sure your area is clean. Every night, make sure you put your tools away. Every night, put back your bins and totes and ves-sels in an orderly fashion. I can't do it all by myself." Danny made a twirl in the middle of the hallway and said, "Alright?" and smiled, showing his missing teeth. Maybe Danny sensed this, so he said to one of the African temps as a diversion, "You gotta smile more!"

The workers laughed, since they knew that guy never smiled. But then the moment was gone, and Danny became the center of attention in the white hallway.

"Let's go to work," he said, so they did. Tomorrow, they would again.

THE APPMAKER

Right after finishing with a moist sweep of the letter "R," our man jumped out of his folding chair. Apps. He could develop apps again!

"No. No. Not apps," he moped. "Everybody is doing apps now." And our man almost sat back down, but instead he kept upright in a sloped posture, pacing around his stale-smelling apartment all dejected. After only a few trips back and forth, he brightened again as he thought, "What about becoming a blogger? I have opinions like everyone else."

Problematically, our man could not write to save his life. Then it hit him, so much so a surge of warm energy foamed up his insides and erupted out of the top of his head. Become someone who cleaned houses by licking them! That was it. The idea of a lifetime. Why hadn't he thought of it before?

Many times our man had done the thing one does when one is bored and unimaginative and can't think of what to do next, the thing where you put your head next to your computer keyboard and examine the dust and hair that has managed to fall between the keys and start to brush away some of the dust with your finger, only going so far because your fingers are too fat to shimmy their way between the keys, so you stick your tongue out and start to lick the dust from the crevices, and it tastes bitter, but there is something to it, you admit to yourself, something nice and satisfying in getting rid of that dust and hair and food debris. Only God knows how long the stuff has been there, and maybe the hair isn't yours, and it might get stuck in your mouth and make you gag, yet despite all that, licking the areas between the keys is the thing you have chosen to do. Yes, all the decisions you have made so far in life led you to the point where the thing you do is lick your keyboard, and that's not great, but at least you're doing something not just sitting in your chair staring at your computer screen wondering how you will fill the next few moments that remain of your pitiful life.

Our man did this almost every day, trying to think of how to spend the rest of his time on earth in a way that would lead him to a place where he did not have to constantly think about how he would spend the rest of his time on earth. He did it so much, hardly any dust or hairs remained between his keys.

"A squeaky clean keyboard, made spotless by the human tongue. The very first mop," he wrote in the description on Craigslist.

Our man thought it clever, to describe the tongue like that. He even included a picture of himself wearing short jean shorts—Levi's that were out of style years ago, from deep in his drawer—along with brown loafers with tassels, and a blue t-shirt that might have fit him in his early twenties but at the point where he put up the ad for cleaning services "with a lick and a smile" it was so tight it showed off his nipples—whether erect or soft it did not matter—and caused his armpit fat to bulge as it stretched around his pectoral muscles and made another fold, acting as the small ball to the big tire around his middle that transformed him into a snowman.

Even after seeing the mirror selfie, our man did not become discouraged. He just submitted the ad, set his eyes on his television, and waited for the phone to ring. That day, our man played his games with an unusual amount of hope. Normally they passed the time in a way our man would describe as "pleasant." Though down beneath the breezy, time-melting nature and serotonin-releasing bits was a disconcerting truth, that whenever our man's hero died, forcing him to start a quest over, a deep and unsettling disquiet came over his soul, and he sensed himself making a grave mistake in spending so much time fighting fake battles to achieve illusionary success.

Our man kept playing, but this time whenever he failed he would remember the licking idea and smile inwardly and feel almost bad for all the noobs out there teabagging. All they had, when they rested their head on their *Call of Duty* pillowcase at night, was the knowledge of when they woke in the afternoon there would be a cold Mountain Dew in the fridge and maybe mom would have a casserole of ground beef with creamed corn and green beans, and they could slurp and gulp for the evening wrapped in basement darkness, interrupted only by the flashes as they anticipated those sudden twitches of adrenaline after the transitory high of finishing off an opponent with a combo so deft it almost made them want to fap.

Yes all those things were great, but shallow, our man suddenly knew. Like he had grown in twenty minutes as much as he'd failed to grow in the last twenty years, all the way from the pimply, greasy solitary life of fifteen to the fat, bald solitary life of thirty-five. Now he was a man with the blueprints for a prosperous future, one where he could make money and attract a wife and support children by cleaning houses by licking them. The key to the idea was in its simplicity.

Several days passed, and after work each day our man stuck by his phone, waiting for the first call. He was just about to start worrying that perhaps his idea had not been a great idea when the phone rang.

"Hello," our man answered, cheery yet nervous.

"Hello," a voice replied. "You're the one who cleans houses with his tongue?"

"Yes I am!" our man said, erring on the side of jubilant. "How can I help you today?"

"I need you to come over and lick me clean."

"That can be done!"

"Good," the customer said. "Be here at nine tonight. Don't be late."

"I won't," our man said. "Where do you live?"

But there was only the sound of the dial tone. Seconds later, a text with an address. Another relief. Far too happy to be aware of any details, our man got dressed, ready to start the first chapter of his so far forgettable life.

Our man took deep breaths in his beaten-up Chevy Malibu. Not the reinvented Malibu or the old souped-up classic, a conventional maroon car, the kind someone who has trouble keeping up on insurance payments might have. Our man's spirits betrayed its dumpy veneer. He jumped out beaming, like a college freshman who hops out of her first car after arriving to the county fair with a group of her friends. Now home for the summer and having the time of their lives, they reminisce about their first year away. They are ready to get into a little trouble, but not too much trouble. How could they? They have finished high school, and now with the rules of adolescence lessened they can stay out as late as they want and eat corn dogs and cotton candy and sip a little vodka as they talk about boys and maybe go skinny-dipping at the local pool later but oh yes they will still call home since they have grown wise in that first year away and know their parents appreciate a call.

That was how our man got out of his Malibu. He strode to the front door of the customer's house, carrying cleaning supplies with him as backup. The job would pay $100 for one hour's work, more than our man made in two days at his social service job where he entered data part-time. Our man was not equipped for a job that required more than thirty hours of dedication. Not unless he found a job as a video game player slash scrolling through his phone looking at pictures of large butts and perky breasts and thick bushes and tan lines on white buttocks, and every time he saw one of those, living a world so separate from his, our man died. Ironically, he also felt compelled to look after perishing in a video game. Dying electronically in a fantasy land always sent an urge to scroll through the millions, and once he found one he liked he'd squeeze his prick until finished then wipe up the mess with a damp towel then go and eat standing up in front of his mostly barren refrigerator as he looked around in space, wondering what else he could do, until he inevitably returned to his game. This had been his life for years, and he was scared of trying to find any other job. The video games depressed him, eating his soul, and the pictures of the women always led him nowhere, but it was his life. It went this way until he thought of the idea while in front of his keyboard for a long time intermittently cleaning it with his tongue of licking houses, and that idea led him up to the front door of a house.

Our man rang the doorbell, holding the cleaning supplies. He had put them in the ad: "a mop and *Clorox* bleach, *Bar Keepers Friend*, *Windex* for glass and *Old English*, all the classics." He could use them all, if need be, but the tongue would be the angle. The house he stood in front of sat in an area to the west of the city, a part where someone in the planning office once put a mall to separate one group from another. In Oconomowoc—no Indians live there any-more—our man knocked on the green front door. As he waited, he thought how strange, that someone would have a green front door.

No one answered, and our man knocked again. The noise echoed deeply this time and soon after was the clicking of heels. It made our man's anus tighten. For just a moment, a figure passed by a slit in the diaphanous curtains and our man saw large breasts, the kind that are intimidating in youth and larger now after childbirth—this house had definitely supported the rearing of children who went to expensive private schools—and also meaty thighs connected to formed buns, the kind kept up through years of yoga. The matron of a house like this would do yoga to keep up appearances.

Our man thought he must be dreaming. The afternoon before he watched a mature woman, maybe in her mid-thirties, give vigorous satisfaction to a bald man by choking on his oversized member, and our man experienced flashbacks from time to time, a quick picture in his mind of those he watched slamming against each other, and that must have been it. The door slowly opened. She was better than what he thought he had seen.

"A little greedy, aren't we?" she said.

Our man did not know what to say in return. She wore next to nothing. Her bra was a series of interconnected straps with no cups, and her nipples poked through. Her underwear, our man noticed, was a light green, just like the front door. Could she have planned that?

"Coming in?" she asked. Our man stumbled forward. He wanted to get in before someone could put a stop to his waking dream.

The house smelled of lavender. What does lavender smell like, our man wondered. It must be something like this. The woman stood in front of him with the interlay around her breasts, and her nipples peeked out between the black straps that held up her two heavy teardrops. She had such large nipples. He thought, *I could stare at those forever.*

"Are you going to do your job, or what?" she asked.

"Oh, yes. Yes yes. Let me get to it," our man said, his body going two directions at once. "Which room would you like done first?"

"Room," the woman said. "I want my pussy licked, boy, for one hour, like you said in the ad you'd do." She rolled her panties down with her long arms over her thick legs, kicking them aside with the knife edge of her heel.

Our man went flush red, dropping his vacuum handle. While attempting to grab it he dropped it again, and it hit the floor with a short cracking sound, a sort of *bap*. He picked it up as he started to bumble, "Miss, I'm sorry, you must have misread. You're beautiful, don't get me wrong." Our man could not stop staring at her nipples. Even the air in the room made him more excited. "But my ad says I lick rooms clean."

"Rooms?" the woman said. Her crotch was shaved. "That's stupid. Why would you lick rooms clean." Just to check anyway, she picked up an iPad from an end table beside a recliner in a vast living room with high ceilings as our man dreamed of satisfying her as much as those in the videos who seemed so satisfied when the men with their shorn testicles did their work. They maintained an erection for so long, seemingly endlessly if they needed to, giving everything the other ever wanted until they could not take anymore, then they gave them more.

The woman scrolled through her tablet, looking for the ad, and our man watched, mesmerized. How the universe opens up chances for those who make their own way. Fortuna was spinning her wheel in our man's direction. The geometry of the one standing there, wearing nothing except for a pair of black high heels and a confusing but ultimately alluring bra, made our man sure of that. Even if he had to leave with nothing, he would be able to use the image of her for months, years if she let him take a picture.

Shoot, he thought then. His phone was still in his Malibu.

"Are you fucking kidding me?" the woman said, putting down the tablet and looking at our man with a confused disgust.

His instantly dropped. Lick rooms as a way of cleaning them? Who does that? This is what you get in this world for trying to make a way for yourself, it chews you up and spits you back without ceremony. Forgets you for years and does not blink an eye. Fortuna's wheel had been spinning the other direction the whole time.

"I'm sorry, ma'am," our man said. "Sorry for the confusion." He leaned over and picked up his cleaning product caddy. In his other hand was the vacuum handle.

"Wait a minute," the woman said, lowering one hip, putting her hand on the other. "You can still get paid if you want to. I can guide you if you're having trouble. Your tongue must be used to a workout."

For a second our man toyed with the idea of telling her this was, in fact, his first job cleaning houses. Maybe even tell her he was a virgin when it came to licking houses *and* a virgin when it came to bringing a woman to fruition. In his years of online dating he performed the act plenty of times but never was he sure what to do exactly. Spell the alphabet with your tongue, make broad strokes, spit, incorporate fingers, create suction, always use a flat tongue. He read tips in forums, and maybe once a girl lifted her hips up toward his mouth and seemed to want more, but never did he feel, as he imagined one was supposed to, a full release. The problem is that he was never close enough with any online partner to ask what they really wanted.

A problem for another night, our man decided. One hour seemed like the perfect amount of time to get it right. So he dropped his cleaning supplies and made a mad rush, like tunneling to the beginning of time, to the very first ember of life.

Our man drove home with a sore jaw and a happy heart,. During his time ensconced in her, the woman never asked our man to take off his clothes, to "whip it out and smack me in the face with it," as they say in the videos he watched. She just lay back on the recliner and instructed our man with her voice or her hand. And with that our man was well pleased. He did not ask for more. After the hour, his tongue so raw it chafed, she simply told him to get up.

"Get your shit and leave," she said, placing money on the end table. Then she strode away down the long hallway with framed paintings on either side of her. He heard the shower start before getting out the door.

Her smell drenched his car over the fast food and his flatulence, and it made our man beam. For some time he had lived alone and for some time marinated in his own juices. Then on the day he would have expected his car to reek of the cleaning products he'd bought for his new business, it smelled like a grown woman at the height of her powers with a lavish home and a rich husband who was off making deals or hitting the links or whatever it was rich people did. She boasted dominating breasts the size of melons and areoles the size of saucers, with nipples like thimbles, all pricked and lovely. These were the miracles afforded to men who made a way for themselves, of that our man was sure as he drove in his out-of-date Malibu with the steering out of alignment.

At home in his one-bedroom apartment, our man got undressed, went to the shower, and took care of himself. In his younger days he could go for hours. Back when he lived with his parents, during summer breaks from college he could click from picture to picture of busty teens who seemed innocent yet developed, squinting until his eyes turned red at thumbnails of the ones who looked like someone who could be his girlfriend. Holding on to the tip of his member, as if trying to put a lid on a volcano. It was just too good to see their excruciatingly perfect forms. How badly he wanted one of them to be his.

Years later, after returning home from the house with the green door, our man had hardly undressed before unleashing his seed onto the fiberglass bed of his tub. Turning on the water, a stream pushed away the viscous cream, and as it got sucked down for good our man wondered if there was something wrong with his prick. Many times during sex, back when he somewhat regularly entertained women, he'd worried about it. He just thought it was supposed to be able to go for a longer time, and that he had maybe done something in his youth to stunt its abilities, like when he used his mom's back massager on his crotch over his shorts. The ones in the videos our man watched could pump so hard without ever needing to finish. The length of time our man could go before spurting did not seem adequate. There were exercises for that, he had heard. They can help, but the sensation of inwardly lifting his pelvis always made him uncomfortable.

In the shower is often where doubts intensified. But that day, after being with the woman in the green underwear who stripped out of them like nothing and leaned back like a goddess for over an hour, our man exuded the confidence of an African bushman, with a member so long and proud it dangled between his thighs out of the coarse hairs he had not maintained since before he online dated and failed miserably.

Dried off and dressed, wearing a pair of gray cut-off shorts and no shirt, our man went to the couch, and instead of turning on the television and playing his video games and looking at pictures of undressed hipsters sucking on each other's breasts or gape-mouthed Vegas blonde waitresses with dark roots wailing—often with three or four members filling up every orifice—our man put music on his turntable, which he had not used in, well, when was the last time another human breathed between his walls?, and he thought, yes really thought, about what his next steps should be.

In the age of apps, our man began to believe his face to face business could be an empire. A new age of women getting what they want. Yes, all women. And so too our man.

The next day our man went to the bathroom, but not for his usual morning routine of standing naked at the edge of the tub, poised with one foot on the ledge and the other planted on the bathmat with phone in hand, scrolling through forms with moist skin taking photos into mirrors or on top of hard bodies with no hair, the nubile college-aged nymphomaniacs can never get enough of, no, our man left his phone on the nightstand. He would not release his genes to let them be drained inconsequently. Maybe, as a pronatalist might argue, one of his swimmers was more powerful than the water from a million showers. Today, he groomed himself.

Our man took a moment to really look at himself in the mirror and take stock of what he had become. In the naked light he could not blame the one with the breasts and nipples in the palatial house who had lain back for over an hour. He got why she would not want his heaving body on top of her and his prick inside her manicured, verdant opening, no matter how slippery and inviting he might make it. Our man could understand how she could resist, seeing himself in the mirror. When did he start looking like this?

For many years our man did not look at himself in the mirror. Too painful to take it in, all the weight and the balding. The bags under the eyes, cutting a deeper line in our man's face with every year. The sagging chin killed our man. He could feel the jiggling up and down his neck. All of it was terrible to think of, but that day after not masturbating first thing in the morning our man saw the best of everything. Hell, he thought, *I am younger than a lot of guys.* Perhaps he could even say he was more virile than a fair number of forty-year-olds, a healthy grouping of fifty-year-olds, and almost all of the over-sixty-year-olds. Those geriatric cases dealt with issues like incontinence and hollow bones and graying skin, and many didn't even want sex, much less could they make themselves useful for it.

"That's so much better," our man thought, reveling in the recent memory of the woman with the pale breasts and long nipples. He had enjoyed a very close picture of her, like an hour-long anatomy lesson for a medical student.

It was good, our man reasoned, to be relatively young. To be in one's mid thirties, whatever age our man happened to be—he often forgot what year exactly—to wake up and have energy and want to touch oneself and afterward be able to ambulate and put on clothes for the day without trouble, to be able to run and jump if one wanted, to still have dreams! They had been buried for so long. Now our man dug them out and dusted them off to find they had deteriorated, but were not completely gone.

Our man had heard it said that it didn't matter what a man looked liked, only what kind of status he accrued. To think, then, of status rolling in with the new idea, bequeathed like when Moroni gave Joseph Smith the plates, or when Adam's finger touched God's. That kind of heavenly magic, flowing directly from the woman through the channels of her vagina and right to our man's lips. Like a psycho-tropic fluid, informing his brain. In this brave new world, our man would need to look his best. He could stand to lose a few pounds.

Do people ever actually lose weight in real life? he thought, sucking in his gut in front of the mirror. He had tried and failed many times, and saw the process of losing weight as an adult like one sees the Loch Ness Monster. It was vanity of vanities, getting into better shape in the advanced years. Our bodies, he knew, are in a state of atrophy starting at puberty, and our man was well past puberty. He stood up straight and sprayed a cold line of shaving cream on his shoulders, rubbing the menthol-infused gel into a foam until it covered the dark hair of his upper arms, stopping at the lighter blonde wisps on his forearms, and he began to shave. It took some time—our man smacking his razor more than once into the goopy, hairy pile of water in his sink—but eventually he finished the job. His reward after wiping off with a used towel—damp from showers—was two rubbery shoulders, one left and one right, both capable of deceiving a person into thinking those shoulders had been like that all the time.

"So nice and glabrous," she might say.

Our man twisted to see his back. He didn't have anyone to put on the sulfuric balm to dissolve the hairs and transform his back into the kind of back a man in his mid- to late thirties could be proud of and show a millennial in a Tinder affair. Our man needed to stave off having the back of a dad in his mid-forties who did not have time for manscaping.

She had been gone for almost three years, and that seemed kind of unbelievable to our man as he tried to reach around and shave himself. It had been that long? What had he done in the interim? What about everything they once planned?

Our man shook off the past and got his nose trimmer and started to clean up what he could reach. The hair was probably too long. The cheap, battery-powered machine, with its tiny saws going back and forth, would never be enough for the hairy gnarls. Still our man fought and did the best he could and even resolved with himself, once he mowed it down some, that he would go to a salon and have it professionally maintained. Maybe his ass too, and the hole, why not. How many secrets the world held beyond the staid efficiency with self-released semen stains everywhere. All the things our man once put off and never would again.

But the problem of bills. Food and rent and cable and internet and insurance. The problem of getting up and going to work. Even the day after our man cleaned up—shaved his shoulders and his back, leaving stubble in some spots and tufts of hair higher up on his scapula where he could not reach—he needed to go to work. Satisfying people by licking their most intimate spots for money did not sustain him yet. He had yet to take the right pictures of himself in the mirror to entice new customers, better-looking even than the rich woman with the breasts and nipples who leaned back on her plush couch and used her hands to guide.

Monday morning. Time for the office job. Our man worked many jobs before his latest in an office. So many, in fact, that at this point in his life it was pointless, he believed, to maintain a resume to connect with employers online like his peers did. His history evolved so sloppily and had become so scattered, he knew no one would be looking for a guy who had worked at factories but before that lived for a year as a houseparent at a group home in rural Nebraska, then after the group home but before the factories in other Midwestern cities dabbled in transportation dispatch for a company that delivered boxes in the Pacific Northwest, then was employed at a bookstore but not as a bookseller, just someone who unloaded books and put them on carts with other books, then after that spent time at another factory driving a forklift and cutting steel on a shear.

That kind of resume would not do for any employer who made apps. The most reputable employers, with offices repurposed from old mattress factories, all brick and lofty, who hired kids straight out of private colleges who yearned for life experience and on late nights when no one else lingered in the office, when it was just her, the new hire, and the boss, who wore a gray wool suit with an Italian-knit tie and English loafers—he could afford the outfit as the manager of the social media managers—coyly expressed a desire to be spanked like in that movie she saw in junior high. The movie is called *Secretary*, but the social media neophyte is not a secretary. She is a woman, fully realized, who gets her own money and a Mini Cooper but still wants a man to see the new things she bought from Agent Provocateur.

Those people are found at jobs where people like our man worked. He would need a time machine to get that kind of job; then and only then would he know enough to leverage himself into a position where he could be in charge of the social media coordinators and manipulate those younger men or women into staying a little bit late. Even the hope of an interview for a job like that had melted and petered out like a candle's wick into a poof of a fantasy. For a while, years ago, our man dreamed of working in advertising. He had taken journalism classes in college.

"I would have just focused," he often whined to himself. "Not taken the easy and wide road of sociology. If there had just been a plan!"

Finally then, a plan, the licking business, and work to be done. In the meantime our man sat down in his chair inside his gray cubicle in the office. Two long rows of them.

Cheryl and Tammy took up the cubes in the front and lorded over everyone. On his first day he could remember Cheryl whispering loudly to Tammy about the bits of data he'd missed. Tina shouted over the cubicles about what kind of panties were the best ones to buy. Nina talked about her heavy period. Maxine came in each morning wearing dark sunglasses and four or five bags strapped over her shoulder. Tracy wore no shoes and ate chicken wings for lunch every day. Mona was in the cubicle behind our man and daily needed help getting logged on to her computer. Celina always reported to no one in particular how hungry or cold she was. Terry, the one other male in the office, sang R&B songs out of tune and mostly talked with Mona about all the girls who wanted him.

Each day of work blended into the distant background of our man's life. Correcting errors, typing words and numbers into a spreadsheet for hours. Hours of inputting information into a database so people who had been given a bad deck could be given money from the state so they could try and raise children who had been abandoned by their parents. Some say there is only one set of cards that God gives each of us, and there is no point in trying to ask for another.

Our man did not want to believe that. He sat in his cubicle and typed in the data absentmindedly, dreaming of the woman in her straps and underwear and heels, her head tilted back, her tongue licking her lips. He thought of how his life would be without the drudgery and heartbreak. Now older, the invisible path his life had gone down could veer off of at any point. Flipping open another file, our man clicked over to his email and looked at his ad with the new pictures. Yes, any direction was possible now.

───── ❧ ─────

Time went by, and our man began to lose little bits of the memory of the woman in straps. Another day started like it always had for the past depressing years: pelvis pointed toward the tub, looking at forms. Work, boring work, then in the evening instead of checking his email for an answer to the new ad, that little letter in his inbox to use as a rocket to another planet where his life was perfect, our man played his video games, leveling up his characters, using that reward as the carrot his brain needed to continue living. That day, the receptionist snapped her fingers at our man to get his attention, and Maxine, with her four bags, wearing dark sunglasses and drinking a Diet Mountain Dew, came in around noon on the phone, talking to her husband about the schedule for that night.

"I have an appointment at four o'clock, then one at five thirty," our man heard Maxine say, "and then I'll come home and take a shower, like I said, and Mom wanted me to do her hair tonight, but like I said I think I can get her to do another night. Like I said, I'll just come home and take a shower after my appointments."

That same day our man went home and ate pizza then passed out and woke up and went to the shower and positioned himself and began to scroll, searching for wide hips and hairy underarms and big breasts all soapy, when he heard a ding.

"I read your ad," our man read immediately, "and what you're offering sounds intriguing. For introductions, I am a fifty-year-old man and my asshole is aching for a young tongue. I pay cash upon arrival. Discretion is paramount. Send a nude pic of you sticking out your tongue. I'll use this as collateral and destroy it once we are finished."

Standing like a statue, postured at the rim of the tub, our man took his foot down slowly, dazed, though also glad. It would have caught him off-guard to go up to a house, guileless with his cleaners and mop and vacuum and tongue, to find a middle-aged man spread-eagle and waiting. For that much, our man was happy. But as his prick drooped in his hand, becoming so small he could no longer hold it in his palm, just his fingers, his brain no longer sending messages to his prick that soon there would be slapped asses, our man yearned for his normal drab Monday night to be spiced up with an email from a woman. Tan, with puffy nipples, a bit overweight and sick of online dating and experienced, someone who wanted a real love. Our man pondered the other side. He once was friends with someone who said our man landed "in the middle of the spectrum." Our man didn't know what the spectrum was, or that the one who told him was in fact gay himself, our man just knew he liked the female body: the way it moved, the sounds it could produce. Though he could remember well in the longest relationship of his life that he often became grossed out by just the idea of having sex. The thought of it began to cause in him a guttural reaction that eventually caused them to not have sex at all. They would argue when she asked why they never did it, and he would go around it by giving lies. Fights like that added up and ended them, after too long spent furtively pining for new rendezvous with those he saw on the street or at his job or online. That was back when our man taught himself to code and he made an app and he tried to befriend media and marketing types and just the idea of a different person, even a man, seemed, at times, more appealing than the same woman over and over again.

Now in the present, our man reasoned going to a man's house would at least be better than leveling up another imaginary character in another imaginary world. He left the bathroom. Time to level up in life.

—⠿⠿⠿—

Our man sighed as he carried the cleaning supplies to his Malibu. The middle-aged man did not say he wanted anything more than what he asked for in the message, but our man held out hope, and carrying out the cleaning products meant people took his business, and his life, seriously. Our man really wanted to be more than a guy who licked for a living. He once made apps, and apps were saving the world.

While driving, our man heard the preachers of his youth. Being gay meant a sin germ had infected him and caused a "bad" or "wrong" desire. Deep down, something had gone haywire in adolescence, or there had been abuse, if one sought out others of their own gender. Abuse, though, that could not be. Our man enjoyed an idyllic upbringing on a farm, where he played in a sandbox with his imaginary friend Johnny, slid down a Slip'N Slide with his older sisters and friends from the neighboring farm. His parents wanted the best for our man and his sisters, sacrificing and working to prevent the worst of the world while allowing in the best, dressing them in the best clothes they could afford, taking care to make sure their progeny grew up happy, so the next generation had it better than they ever did. It's what every parent wants.

Thinking of his mom and dad, our man began to cry in his car. He would have to do this to become something more than what he was, a guy who worked at a job he hated, masturbated, and played video games to trick himself into thinking he accomplished something each day. Just the night before, Simon and Garfunkel's "April Come She Will" played, a song our man's mother would play on vinyl when he was just a boy. Our man had been so drunk it reminded him of everything up until his licking business.

"And then, of course," our man said out loud in his Malibu, stammering and slobbering like a toddler, "even that stupid idea goes wrong."

Our man pounded his fists on the steering wheel, then immediately realized how incredibly self-involved what he had said was. Even our man was embarrassed by our man, and he did not believe in suicide. No matter how bad things got, it always seemed to him a selfish act, like a final plea for more online favorites. There were the mentally ill, those who heard voices and saw invisible monsters and had to repeat actions until they made a rut in their living room floor, those who lived with more guilt than they could carry. Their endings could be rationalized. For people like our man, those with all their toes and limbs who lived with a mind that worked at its full capacity—even if he seemed unable to mine any useful ore out of it—suicide was a coward's way of ending existence. It was his personal theory, at least.

Our man told himself to stop crying and get inside the house, less impressive from the outside than the woman's with the breasts and nipples. A hint of danger lingered on the dark lawn, unlit by any recessed lamps. Our man took a deep breath and got out and dutifully hauled the cleaning products from his Malibu to the front door. Heroically, he thought, lying to himself. In his mind, he was ready to do what he came to do, probably, he thought, on the beige carpet of a house a single person did not buy and would never sham-poo because he did not have the money or the energy.

Setting down the vacuum and the broom and the all-purpose jani-tor caddy, a Rubbermaid, our man rang the doorbell. Online, the ad said the caddy could securely hold up to eight thirty-two-ounce spray bottles, and its ergonomic handle allowed for conformabil-ity, though our man had yet to utilize his tools. It was more deco-ration, like a useless ornament, a prop next to the pile of meat that opened to masticate via the slithering wet muscular hydrostat which mostly in its life had been used to chew food. Very shortly, it would venture into unfound territory.

Finished, our man packed up his cleaning products and left sheepishly. Hustling to his car, cleaning caddy jangling, he threw his vacuum into the back, causing a crash that sounded like something broke. He dropped the rest of the products haphazardly on the front seat and jetted around to the driver's. Our man put several pieces of spearmint gum in his mouth to wipe away the memory. It could be that our man was more interested in men than he thought he was, or maybe he was just out of options, since every decision he made up until that point put him in a spot that spiraling his tongue in and around another's man asshole had become the only thing left to do if he wanted to be something more than a guy who played video games and looked at videos of bodies being used as holes and worked at a job he resented. The other choices were to move home or kill himself, and neither were any way to treat aging parents.

Our man drove home through Milwaukee, the last place he would have dreamed of living. He had moved there after meeting her years before at a wedding in the South. He knew of her, and she knew of him, through the mutual friends who got married in Charleston in a lavish wedding that featured a station for hand-rolled cigars and all the free top-shelf alcohol you could drink and food you find at a high-end tapas restaurant. From what our man knew, the groom did not love the bride, just the idea of loving her and someone loving him, of being somewhere where every day someone else cared enough to wonder what time he would be home and ask what was for dinner each night. It was much better than going home and warming up three or four or five brats with deadly nitrates and eating them on generic buns with chemicals baked into them and drinking a Coke or two or three then having explosive diarrhea then coming back to bed and taking off all his clothes and being nude on the bed after a day of unhappy factory work, just sort of swimming his legs with phone in hand, scrolling through the latest news in the tech world so that when our man finally made an app to propel him out of his lot, he'd be ready, even if mostly he looked at *Tumblr* posts of trim yoga teachers on beaches wearing bikinis that rode up their large asses until he went to the shower and expunged himself of the desire.

Our man drove to his efficiency in a Rust Belt city by the lake. His adult apartment was not unlike his first place right after college in Sioux Falls, where in approximately the same arrangement he put the bed in the "living room" near his desk and separated it with a couch. No one ever told our man it would always be so gloomy in Wisconsin. He had lived in Seattle, where the weather fit the mood, but the unexpected similar conditions in the Midwest seemed grayer when compounded by the heavy beer, thick cheese, and a sense that the greatest thing in life would be to live through a Super Bowl win then the next day play video lottery in a smoky casino. Our man drove, sure that he would never see the sun shine again, as other drivers got very close to his bumper on the wide-open interstate then passed him like in a NASCAR race. Our man wanted to honk or flip the bird, or something, but instead did what he always did, spoke a derogatory word under his breath and shook his head.

What happened to do unto others, our man bemoaned to no one in the cold interior of his Malibu. He could not see the sun or the moon. Almost midnight, he would have to be at work in the morning.

Our man's inbox went dry. Just as well. He did not have the internal fortitude to go out and satisfy anyone by licking them. It became very cold in the city by the lake, colder than anywhere else in the country, which made our man wonder why he continued to live where he lived. Arizona existed, Florida too. Being a homeless person in those climates seemed preferable to being an employed person in a tundra where the sun never came out and the only recreation was eating cheese.

Sitting in front of his computer with no hope, our man forgot his dreams. He subsumed himself in liquor and fast food and online pictures of slick flesh rubbing, in gif form and, when drunker, video. When not doing that, he played video games, and when our man's character died he would drink and return to the screen of his phone, where he brought up fit bodies in states of undress and arousal, amateur selfies in bathrooms, ones our man could not have had in even his greatest of years. Too timid and skinny, our man, compared to the large confident football men of college, or after, those who lifted heavy weights at the YMCA in Sioux Falls, drank protein shakes, wore visors on their heads and puka shells around their necks, those who had gone on spring breaks all four years previous and now at 23 worked as pharmaceutical representatives.

Women splattered all over the internet. Our man did not stop and wonder how many had been uploaded out of jealousy. Our man got busy pleasuring his mind and body, drenching himself in the serotonin, and did not think of any unpleasant scenarios. After work each night he finished on the wood floor of his dirty apartment and did not bother to clean it up. He'd then pass out on the couch with the fluid oozing on his stomach, which eventually became crunchy. In the morning he went to work hungover, then came back home again to do it all over. For sustenance he ordered pizza or takeout, and his efficiency began to develop the smell of decaying human and greasy food. With the remains of pizza boxes and dirty clothes, his place looked to be more or less the opposite of what he purported to provide in his advertisement for "A Good Licking House." In the rare moments when our man allowed silence, suicide began to seem like a real option.

After nearly two months of that, a good while after our man licked a man, he got the email that saved his life. She went by Aurora ---and she sent a picture in her very first message. A gamer, she said, and that immediately got our man's juices flowing, then with his next breath he was sure it was a joke, the kind of cruel one they play online, like when they call 911 and have a SWAT team invade a stranger's house.

"I think your ad is hilarious," she, the presumed catfisher, said. "You lick for a living? For real? You should come over and lick my house. Also, I call my house my pussy. Just so you know."

She wore a Wonder Woman costume that did its best to cover her breasts, though even if the garment tried twice as hard it could not have done the job. She sent her backside too, and it was so eye-watering to our man, like a thick piece of meat, two hams poking out of the blue bottom piece with white stars, and the gold ties at the sides that in one second could be undone and slipped off.

Our man sighed. What an awful joke someone played on him. Luckily, he was drunk. If sober, he would not have replied.

"Sure, babe. I'll lick you like a cat," and along with that message he sent a picture of his cat, which at that moment was licking itself (our man owned a cat and it roamed around his place and lived self-sufficiently).

Minutes later, another email. Aurora without a top, covering her breasts with one arm and with the other taking the picture while smiling the most genuine smile, as if what our man had done really made her happy. At the bottom was her phone number, with a peach and a cat-with-hearts-for-eyes emoji.

"Meow me later," she wrote.

Dear God, it didn't make any sense. Though what about love does?

———⟀———

A new outfit would be needed. Aurora could very well be perfect, our man dreamed, though who can really tell these days, he also thought, with the possible angles one can utilize with a phone, making any part of the body look like any other part, as fresh or long or hard or voluminous or thick as we always imagined others would see us. This is what our man's generation had started doing, creating profiles to depict themselves as they wished the world saw them. They invented a place to do so, believing it to be the dream of every other who ever lived before. In the past, only royalty had such royalties.

So off he went to buy new clothes for the first time in honestly he could not remember how long, to a department store with the express purpose of looking good. Now he would have to come face to face with his face. In the past that brought such disappointment that our man would get depressed for a good several hours after seeing what he had evolved into: a sagging, mostly bald, wide human being, with dark circles under his eyes and long lines on his face and a chin so bulging it doubled, all of it badly haunting our man and leading him to think he had either been adopted or cursed with a genome no one else on his fair-skinned Nordic mother's side, nor his dark and handsome Germanic father's side, could be traced back to and found. So, rather than shop, our man opted to wear the same clothes for as long as they could be sustained. Four work shirts for the office, two pairs of khaki pants, and on the weekends a pair of jeans and a gray or navy sweatshirt, to hide some of his girth, along with a pair of sturdy boots, to give him what he hoped was a more rugged appearance. Our man hoped meeting Aurora would draft in a newness, like a flue opening up the air in a chimney, puffing out the old winter soot of stagnancy from years of being alone. The idea for the cleaning service had been a good one, after all, if Aurora turned out to be everything.

But even before he got out of his Malibu in the mall parking lot, self-hatred crept up his throat. Our man tried to bat it down as he exited his late-model sedan covered in salt from the winter, trucks and vans racing past him, but it came back just as strong. The couples and black youths, overweight families, and heavily make-upped throngs did not seem to notice our man's belly tightening as he walked closer in the biting cold to the one store in the mall he knew to be good. His previous lady, long gone, had said so, and our man understood she knew more about fashion and languages and the world in one of her fingers than he would in his whole life.

One time they went shopping, our man and his one-time lady, they went to the same mall where our man now went to prepare for Aurora. Back then on the escalator, our man patted his lady on the back through her puffy coat, and as soon as he saw in the distance the sign for Levi's, he told her he did not want to shop. How impossibly meaningless, he thought, to spend money on clothes, since he always shrunk them in the dryer or got too fat, and the little money he did have he wanted to save, as he was already not paying rent and every penny he spent brought him closer to asking his parents for money again, or worse, his lady's parents.

All of that came back from all those past years. On the way to the men's section, past the displays of dizzying perfumes where women in blazers offered tutorials, past the bras and underwear on dead-faced mannequins, sliding past the one employee helping a man with a gold watch who smelled heavily of cologne and probably had a good job in an office where a receptionist offered free bottles of water, our man did not touch one single garment and continued on the hard-surfaced walkway. He did not drift to where the clothes waited on silver racks and on tiered displays under tasteful lighting. He went in a big loop to the front of the store and out the side entrance of the mall and back to his car.

There, staring in his rearview mirror, our man took off his stocking hat. Never in his life had he purposefully recorded his baldness, as his friend did in a series of pictures our man accidentally saw while snooping around for nude pictures of that friend's ex-girlfriend. The file our man found was titled, "Look How Fucking Bald I Am," and contained pictures at all sorts of angles that documented the loss of coverage. Our man's strategy was one of avoidance. With the family pictures that inevitably captured him at his most bald, he would skim just long enough to see that yes, he existed that Christmas, then never look again.

In his car, after leaving the mall with no clothes, our man decided to be honest with himself. To be as nude as he could be. He removed his hat on an gray afternoon and looked in the rear-view mirror and thought for a second that he saw a ghost. Driving back empty-handed, he could only calm himself by thinking over and over, *what does a ghost need with clothes?*

With much less confidence than he would have had following a successful trip to the mall, our man set out to meet Aurora for what he was sure would be their last meeting. Having no new outfit, he left his apartment wearing what he always wore when he went places where he thought attractive people might be: jeans, gray sweat-shirt—in years before he'd worn a collared shirt underneath, but the look had faded in popularity—and boots, once the more ubiquitous chukkas but in the time of Aurora more expensive, with a "moc-toe." though they were old and beginning to look clunky and worn.

Our man parked near Aurora's apartment building and banged his head on the steering wheel of his Malibu. Crusts and crumbs of ancient lonely meals had collected in the middle console. Leaning forward, he licked the dash, then took a long drink from his flask of whiskey. It was enough to make a person choke, but our man's tolerance was significant, and he kept it in. Taking a piece of gum, he chewed it violently for a minute or two. Without looking in the mirror, he went to her door.

———— ❦ ————

Aurora on the floor next to our man, asking, "Have you ever done anything like that before?"

As if every day someone asked him if they could "suck his cock," as if he every day watched a beautiful woman take off her American-flag-printed underwear, and with them gone rub deeply into her fatty groin, cooing as if she had been waiting for our man her whole life, and when done working herself, her breasts pushing themselves out of a flimsy top, put her whole entire mouth on what our man had, and it hardly took more than a few times to make him shoot it all, as if she had been waiting for that like water from an oasis after walking for years in a dry desert.

When our man arrived an hour before, Aurora opened the door in the same outfit as her pictures, with tall, high-heeled boots. She right away grabbed his crotch and led our man to her bedroom, only a room away since she lived in a humble apartment, but with a plush couch and a good-sized television and rows and rows of video games, our man noticed quickly. Everything clean, with framed posters of old movies. In her bedroom, hardly anything, just white sheets and a brass bed frame, a dresser and a jewelry box. The room heaved with the weight of someone in control who made countless men helpless.

Lying next to each other, Aurora wiped up the last bits of miasma from her lips, like one would do after drinking water from a fountain.

"I haven't," our man said, his pants on the floor, socks on. "Have you?" For a second, he thought, *Is this real life?* He worried he might be part of a graduate school thesis. They stood behind one of those two-way mirrors as proctors with clipboards examining the two on the bed. A research group for a new genre of homemade films.

"Not really, no," Aurora said. He wanted to ask, as it seemed appropriate, why she had replied to his ad and really, how many times had this happened? But our man stopped himself, remembering his days as an online dater and the lesson he'd learned, that one should never ask questions. Always act as if you don't care about anything. Don't have feelings. Be a robot.

"I like your place," our man said, and she shifted her body. She put one of her legs over our man's stomach and one between his legs, like a scissor. Our man felt her as she nuzzled up against him.

"Thank you," she said. "That's so sweet. Did you want to play some video games?"

This all had to be a joke, so our man laughed, but later on Aurora's couch, she in shorts so short they seemed like another joke and a shirt so tight our man wasn't sure if one could technically call it a shirt—more like body paint—she put down her controller, having intermittently during the game tugged at our man to see if he was waking up, and took him in her mouth. This time, he lasted longer, and before our man finished he told her he was close, and she released herself from his prick.

"Come on my face, please," she said. So that is what our man did.

From the living room just a few minutes our man saw Aurora bending over to put a pizza in the oven, and he thought, with a satisfied tackiness in his balls, that this could not be happening.

"Did you want to get high?" our man heard from the kitchen. Seconds later, Aurora brought out the pizza and a soda, filled to the brim with ice. She asked how he wanted his drink.

"Yeah," our man said. "Sure."

"Perfect," Aurora said and sat down and opened the drawer of the coffee table. Inside was a tin. In the tin, a Ziploc bag. A wave of strong green flower came over the room.

"It's really good stuff," she said, packing the bowl and sprinkling the ground crystals on top. She gave our man the first crack, and it made him cough, which made her smile. Still smiling, she took her hit. "I'm so glad you're here," she said. "I needed this."

Our man took a large hit. He did not want to say it, so as to avoid sounding eager, but he thought what Aurora said might be the truest thing he'd heard in his entire life.

Driving home the next morning beaming. At his studio, our man heard his cat meowing, so he dumped the remainder of food from the messy bag, spilling out in a corner of the kitchen, and went to the couch. Not to play video games or look at naked women in the back of fake taxi cabs needing to find a way to pay the fare, but to create. To really *create* for the first time in a long time.

Years before, the idea had been for an app "to make a difference." Not a micro-transactional game or a knock-off scam that notified users of people nearby who wanted to have sex and eat at the best pho restaurants. No, our man wanted to create an app his grandchildren would be proud to use. The idea, taken not so subtly from the film *Eternal Sunshine of the Spotless Mind*, was to create something that allowed users to zap memories from their brain. All one needed to do was download the app then input the memory he or she wanted to forget and walk through the steps. The only hurdle was incorporating the erasing technology. Our man knew, if he could just get it working up until that point, a med-tech company in Silicon Valley would step up to the plate and supply the rest. Everyone had plenty they wanted to forget. In the present, our man also knew his app could be monetized, and money was what gave status, and status was what would allow our man to have even more women like Aurora.

She said she'd be "going out of town for a bit" and would not be reachable, "so don't freak if I don't get back to you." But her being away would be good, as it would supply the time needed to dust off the old architecture and see what bugs needed fixing and which lines just needed a little tweaking before the VC money came rolling in.

Click clack click clack.

Here is the part where our man sat on his couch—cat wandering in and out—his heels resting on his disgusting coffee table, tapping away. Click clack click clack. Our man's Windows 98 fired on all its remaining cylinders—-our man hated the pomp and circumstance of Apple's OS---and for the rest of that weekend our man got in the zone. It seemed a sure thing he would see Aurora again. How could he not, after such a libidinously pure night? Our man did not stop programming that whole weekend, only taking breaks to call for pizza and to sleep a few hours each night. Not once did he feel the need to stop as a reward for himself, like he had in the past. Not completing the app was what had kept him from greatness, our man was sure of that now. Back in the day he blamed the incestuous community in Mountain View, those he once railed against on his since deleted Twitter account—he could still remember well the victorious feeling of a VC blocking him or a UX designer replying with some variation of "Okay, dude with 109 followers"—but no more. At that moment our man realized it was our man himself stopping our man from becoming what our man wanted. Now in his mid-thirties, it was time for work, and more work. Typing the code, our man imagined himself a young Bill Gates in the garage, and after that he morphed into Steve Jobs driving down the Pacific Coast Highway in a new sports car with a hot transcendentalist, many years younger. Even crushing baldness could not allay our man's progress. In the bathroom after a bowel movement, our man stood in front of the mirror, not blinking or looking away. He did not look like the man he once envisioned himself becoming, nothing like the picture of our man's father at that age, who at forty had a full head of straight, dark hair. But it did not matter. Our man saw the reflection of someone who could have an Aurora, even without an app. Just the promise of creating had transformed our man.

Hell with it, he thought, suddenly sure he could have someone even better than Aurora. Once the app got going and our man started making real money, what did it matter if he was bald? Or even the opposite, he could be like one of those people who grew hair over their whole body like moss. Once our man found success, looks would cease to matter. Like a song our man used to like to sing, where the chorus rang out, "Guys go for looks, girls go for status."

True? Yes. It always had been too, but for the first time in our man's life, its veracity no longer discouraged him.

—◦◦◦—

Our man quit his job where he entered data. He just casually walked in to tell his boss—who was a year older and in charge of the entire office and talked loudly over the cubicles with other women about her period, "clotting and chunks" involved, and who did her nails at her desk and put up wooden wall art that said "Make Today Amazing" and had framed photos of her Pomeranian on her desk and who had worked at the same company for a number of years and made a place for herself and could afford to eat out for lunch every day—that it was over. He did not hesitate either. The days of hesitating were also over.

Officially, he gave two weeks. Our man did not believe in burning bridges, even if he vigorously told himself he would never return. Our man's boss was not as sad as he hoped. She simply said, "We'll miss you," and when the short meeting adjourned our man strode to his cubicle, thinking how the rest of the workers would for the rest of their lives be strapped to their desks, accumulating sad decorations from vacations within the contiguous forty-eight states and pictures of overweight family members, pining and dreaming of a position where they would be allowed to do the least amount of work possible. Forever, our man thought, they will be chained here.

Our man walked out of the soulless building two weeks later. Already he packed up a few things at home. He could leave Milwaukee at any time and did not expect to get his deposit back, so he found no sense in picking up the trash or painting the walls or cleaning the floors. Those jobs were for the working-class now, the blue-collar types whom our man would no longer have to lower his head and deign to join for manna. Packing up a few things---computer, towels, clothes, books on coding— our man got so excited that he forgot all about his cat and somewhere around Colorado, as the monotony of the road set in, it pinged in our man's head that he'd forgotten. At the next rest stop he called the apartment complex manager, identifying himself as a next-door neighbor, saying he heard mewing next door.

Relieved, our man got back on the interstate, letting the road hum beneath him, allowing only the best possible scenarios to run in his brain. Free will existed. He controlled the thoughts that filled his waking consciousness. The elations became so great that the obsessive voices could not break through. He would arrive in Mountain View with his mind unabated. He planned to camp in a forest outside of town and work at a Starbucks. Find a library, perhaps, and use their free internet service, if the coffee shop employees gave him foul looks. Go to a motel once a week or so to get cleaned up, then back out to the wild to commune with nature and appreciate the good his app would soon be doing for the world. All other apps say that's what they do, but our man knew they only made the world worse, bogging it down with unnecessary information about the lives of others.

"We needed to learn how to simplify again," our man wrote with real ink in his first entry of a new journal. "This is what you are selling. Bliss. Total happiness."

Our man wanted it as much as anyone. The thing was, he did not have technology. So he edited and whittled the idea to its core, just the happiness part. Not everyone could handle invasive surgery to eradicate old memories. Going about it holistically was a much better plan. And this way the app could be free for everyone. Part of the trick for the marketing department would be conveying the simplicity. An app that in under a minute perfected inner peace. A state of not wanting any more than the present moment.

Our man went westward, chasing the setting sun, his future ahead of him. Time had passed without hearing from Aurora and up until very recently that sort of ghosting would have driven him to madness, since he sort of felt like finding Aurora was like finding home. He drove, knowing that feeling had been a mirage. How many times it tricked him before. Possibly, he entertained as he drove, meeting her had never even happened. Our man repeated that alternate reality to himself as he camped in a park in Utah. Looking around, it was almost like he camped on Mars. Maybe nothing had happened yet. Maybe everything was about to begin.

Working on an app in a forest outside Silicon Valley in the tranquility of nature, the lush greenery and gentle sounds, the odd woodland creature, though mostly just squirrels and rabbits. Deer, at night. One early morning from inside the tent, our man thought he heard the huffing, snorting breaths of a bear, but it was just the hazy confluence of a dream. During the day he went into town, and at the coffee shop graphed the outline, ditching old attempts if they no longer served the greater whole.

"Work on getting to the core of how to construct a medium that solves the eternal problem," he wrote in his journal. "How does one get from wanting the emotion of happiness to having it? How does one download that feeling at no cost?"

If anything, our man learned, the best companies were free at the start. They made their real money through leasing users' data or by being a thing that everyone wanted a piece of. That ineffable cool factor made the app almost invaluable. "Almost" was a key distinction, though, since there would have to be definable value, and that value would translate into power, and that power would give our man freedom to do whatever he wanted to do for the rest of his life. Once he completed the outline, barely wanting to reveal the idea to himself, much less a lucky bystander getting coffee, our man retreated to a darkened corner of a public library on the outskirts of Mountain View.

"Be damned the extraneous noise," read a note scribbled in the journal in that electric time, "the incessant needy glomming on of so many developers and sycophants."

Our man did not need to rent a space at a place like "BeColony," an office community with pods in a warehouse that was once a feed lot in the early 1900s but had been refashioned to accommodate the plugged-in, bespectacled members of the Twitterverse who wrote for *Medium* and debuted products at Disrupt. Those people could slouch in their bean bags and make their free-to-plays and streaming music services, leeching off the stupidity of the masses, cracking the structure of art and humanity and goodness by making every possible atom in the universe for sale.

Wanting to do good—though secretly below that wanting more to make money—our man sought to etch out a place alongside the other greats in solitude. Like Thoreau, our man lived austerely, using only what he needed, at night sleeping on the ground, not taking more from the land than he gave, and by day secluding himself in the forgotten recesses of a public space, deserted, since all of civilization had forgotten about books. There he was to create the single greatest thing, and he coded. He coded and coded and stopped only to go to the bathroom, nodding his head as he walked by the elderly librarian, then back to his chair to sneakily eat granola bars and drink water out of a Nalgene as he furiously typed, filling in line after line on the screen. With each day it came together more, and with each day our man became more prone to fits of glee, at times becoming so euphoric he'd go outside to the woods, not so far from the library, to scream "Yes!" as loud as he could. The muses shined down upon him. The goddesses of prosperity would follow.

As the app neared completion, our man went to the library less and communed with nature more. He could see in the near future purchasing a modern, domineering home overlooking the ocean. Our man wanted to relish the last moments of the Siddharthan ascetic life. Sitting by his tent, looking up at the great trees, our man came to a peace, and found his Jhāna. He knew he would never again use alcohol or pornography or online dating to fill in the gaps. Real adventures awaited, with real women, and they would not have to drink to have them. He would be able to afford to hire someone whose job it was to secure potent marijuana.

With the app finished, our man packed up his tent, said a final meditative prayer, and drove into town. He rented a room at an expensive hotel, took a lengthy, cleansing shower—the water coming from different angles out of marble—and uploaded his app to the store. The next morning he got back in his car and hit the road to experience this world as a no-name one last time. That kind of thing, our man foresaw, would be an enviable experience that one day he'd yearn for, to be anonymous, so it was best to soak it all in while he could. The only thing our man promised himself not to do was look at stats, comments, or reviews until this vacation for himself had ended. He planned to get tan and lose more weight—he had shed fifteen pounds in the woods by not eating processed foods or drinking—and maybe have one last tryst as a man without status.

He envisioned the interview. Later in life she might say, after someone came knocking at her door, "Oh, yes, come in." And as the interviewer sat down, the subject, now a bit older but still attractive and obviously the kind of woman who was once beautiful, said of when she first met him, "I remember that would have been the spring of 2015. He was a bit heavier than he is now, maybe he didn't have the same stature, you know, the commanding stance that everyone knows—could he have been shorter then?—but he had the same confidence, I think, the fullness of a man. I could tell he'd go on to do great things. Yes, I just knew it, really amazing things."

Before the end there are events to be shared so we better know what our man was like before he became to be the man he is today. One is when he almost got hit in the head with a discus. In the ninth grade our man helped measure the distances of throws at a high school track meet, marking where they landed by running out onto the spring field and putting a yellow tent pylon in the ground. Another classmate scrolled out a special tape measure and yelled out the distance of the throw. One of the times after putting a pylon in the ground, our man must not have been hustling back fast enough, because while leaving the in-bounds area a discus whizzed by his head. Our man figures, at the rate of its descent toward his brain, he would have at best lived through a serious concussion or at worst died. Probably his situation would have been something in between, living the rest of his life in vegetative limbo.

Two, and again in high school, as a freshman at the height of our man's interest in seeing bare breasts and pubic hair, our man found himself on a job, mowing a lawn in straight lines back and forth. That day is when it dawned on our man that it would be a good idea to go across the street to his friend's house. In an instant, our man stopped pushing the mower and left with the job half done, going across the lazy street with the intention of finding a stack of *Playboy*s he knew his friend Nathan to have. Walking in silently through the side door leading downstairs to the wood-paneled walls with Led Zeppelin and Nirvana posters on the walls, not knocking or calling out for anyone, our man heard the stillness. It sent a rush through him and he made a dash to the stack of magazines, picking out the one he'd most wanted to be alone with the time he glanced through it with a group of other boys. Our man sat on Nathan's bed with no contingency plan for if someone came home, then proceeded to work himself up until he spilled it all on the floor. With the deed done, our man grabbed bathroom tissue and blotted at the removable carpet and walked straight out of the house. There was still mowing to be done.

Three, in college our man hardly ever drank. To drink or get drunk would have badly disappointed his parents, and by proxy, himself. In high school, he didn't touch the stuff, but in the two semesters at college before he fully committed his life to Christ---a few years later he also decommitted---our man faked his way through several nights of keggers at off-campus houses with names like "The Jungle House" or "Pussy Tits." One Thursday night our man walked to one by himself, for reasons he did not understand and now certainly could not explain. The only connection being that a guy who grew up with lived there, and maybe there was a girl, since there was always a girl, or the hope of one. Our man showed up with his five-dollar bill and got his red cup and tentatively filled it with light beer once or twice, not knowing the etiquette for doing so. Downstairs with everyone else, he swayed back and forth to the music pumped in by a guy wearing a jester's hat who would probably drop out before the end of that year. By our man's second cup, he was "feeling it." He had to go to the bathroom, and finding a usable bathroom did not seem possible, so our man headed back to the dorms. A short walk across the green grass of the manicured lawn, with the boozy white lamps halfway up the evergreens lighting the path. All of it romantic, our man thinking what it might be like to be accompanied by a girlfriend, but he had only himself and very much had to pee. Problem was, he thought campus police watched his every step, and the desire to not get in trouble was so ingrained in him—deeper than his parents could have ever hoped—that instead of relieving himself behind a tree, in an area so dark only God Himself could have seen, our man decided to keep walking. As he did, he peed his pants. That, he reasoned, solved the problem of having to go and also the problem of getting caught with public intoxication and being pinned with a minor that could ruin his life. Not waiting for it to dry, even though he could have, our man snuck in his dorm, and by God's grace did not meet anyone in the stairwell or come across any of the football players at the end of the hall who kept their doors open and played video games and music at deafening volumes. Almost home free around the corner, our man came head to head with the rest of his floor, the skinny basketball players who smoked weed, the short one who wore Bryant Reeves jerseys, the pimply fan of Relient K, and all the others. Quickly dipping into the utility room, our man for a second thought he'd slipped detection. He waited almost fifteen minutes to let them disperse, but when he got into his room and closed the door, he could hear whispering, with someone saying, "Shit, maybe he just really had to go," followed by loud laughter. Not long after that, our man came to Christ. The two events, he thought at the time, had nothing to do with each other.

Four is when our man was just a little boy, and a friend named Jeremy lived down the street. They played *Mario* and *Duck Hunt* and tackle football and went to the same sleepovers and talked about the love notes they received from girls in their class in kindergarten Jeremy would later marry at nineteen. Ten years before, Jeremy liked doing something our man would never tell anyone about, to come over and lock the door of the bedroom and play "the naked game." It consisted of taking off their clothes and dancing in front of the mirror. To this day, our man is amazed at their unguarded nature.

Five. Our man never told anyone about the whole thing, when he lived with two female roommates for a month in Seattle. He'd spend the night with one and in the morning slink into bed with the other.

Six came before moving to Milwaukee. When living in another Midwest city, our man walked a lonely walk back to his car, blocks away from a movie theater where he'd gone on his own, away from the suburbs where he lived with his landlord. Just as he came out from under branches jutting over the sidewalk, our man spotted another man teetering at the top of a wooden staircase on the side of a rundown house. The man tumbled, going ass over heels before resting at the bottom in a crumple, then he staggered as our man half-jogged up, afraid the whole thing might be a hidden-camera show. Sitting on the cement steps, our man asked if everything was all right. One of the stranger's glasses lenses had fallen out of its frame, so our man set the glasses with the lens near the man and asked again if everything was all right. The man grumbled in return. A cut on his forehead and his white brief underwear was visible, his pants settled somewhere between his waist and his knees. Our man asked again, and this time the stranger shoved our man off. Our man half-stood, frozen in indecision. Daylight in the summer, it seemed like everyone in the neighborhood had gone inside to watch and see what would happen. Our man did nothing, and the guilt stayed with him forever.

Seven happened in high school. It occurred between a boy who would grow up to be a mechanic and one who would grow up to be an electrician. The mechanic boy was always quiet, some-one who came to school with dirty fingernails and talked with a country drawl. The electrician boy had been, for as long as anyone could remember, the prankster class clown—not the witty class clown: class members dedicated loose-leaf tablets to his mishaps, a drawing of when he closed a garage door on his dad, or when he sliced another classmate's hand with a bowie knife. All of the hijinks started off as "jokes" and often ended in disaster. This time, the boys in the non-chorus P.E. class showered after P.E., and the prankster—who always had a girlfriend after the sixth grade and at the age of fifteen drove a Trans Am with "T-tops"—got into it with the boy who would be a mechanic, who spent most of his time working on his trucks and going to drag races. The prankster, built like a man even then, was much more popular than the boy who would be a mechanic, and it was his way to mess with everyone less popular than he. That day he was "playing" with a shampoo bottle, using it as an extra phallus and thrusting his way around the shower. The ones who knew he would do nothing to them laughed, but Tim seemed nervous. It was within the realm of the prankster to do actual damage, and so Tim moved away from the thrusting, which had been hitting Tim's thigh and butt cheek. After a few peaceful moments passing, one of the other football players acting as a distraction and talking to Tim earnestly, the prankster came behind and thrust the shampoo bottle up Tim's anus. Our man wasn't there, but the guys in his class said if you told, you'd get it even worse.

Eight was a happier time. Our man and his youth group went to Minnesota in the spring of 1997. The winter of 1996–1997 had been a brutal one, and the church our man grew up going to went to lend a hand, employing a practical religion. Mennonites spreading their physical gifts, building houses, hoeing crops and digging wells, it all goes hand in hand with the Gospel. The children in the congregation did the same, and that spring the youth group, including our man as a high school boy along with three other boys, traveled in a van with five girls, one of whom had the most developed breasts of all the girls at either the private or public schools.

She and the other girls slept downstairs in the empty house for the week while the boys slept in the room above. The mentors who set up the sleeping arrangement could not have thought of this, but it was Nathan, our man's best friend then, who discovered a vent in their room that led directly into the room below them where the girls changed. For that whole trip, whenever the boys got back to the room, they'd scurry to the vent to huddle around and gaze down in disbelief, then at each other, in a sort of unspoken awe.

Nine. For a good few years before the internet, our man amassed a collection, and if it could be found now—which it cannot, since our man flushed the pages down the toilet in one paranoia-induced purge—it would seem a kind of ancient archive, the Dead Sea Scrolls of '90s women in undress, or as close to undress as one can find in the pages of American fashion magazines of that time. Our man was ravenous and aching to see nudity, just a snippet could send him into a dizzying frenzy of lapsed consciousness and a deep need to be alone rubbing himself. In that time, after receiving the greatest item he ever received, the *Sports Illustrated* swimsuit issue with Kathy Ireland and Elle Macpherson and Rachel Hunter—though Ms. Ireland and her tan breasts led the way—our man began to amass a collection of magazine clippings. He'd tear out pages from magazines in Kmart and Shopko or at Waldenbooks in the mall in Sioux Falls. Sometimes he did the same when staying late at school while his mom corrected papers, looking through *Vogue* and *Glamour* in another room, carefully flipping through each page to find the most revealing pictures. He'd hide the clipping in his waistband under his shirt then hoard it in his closet at home.

Along with the clippings, our man kept an unmarked videotape he snuck downstairs periodically to record—in even just the most narrow of margins of time it took someone else in his family to get from upstairs to downstairs—shows like *Entertainment Tonight*, hoping for the segments when the reporter would go to movie sets where backsides or breasts were quickly censored with a red ribbon. Our man would later, when no one was home, press play on the slowest speed and pause on the grainy millisecond where the program had been remiss to allow a moment of unadulterated skin. Even better were the USA Up All Night movies, which our man could not tape as often since he was not allowed to watch, but he would try his best to get stuff from *Knockouts* and *Bikini Carwash*. Eventually, our man threw out the entire collection, meticulously gathered over years. All the magazine pages, and the two swimsuit issues, both 1994 and 1995, flushed down the toilet. He destroyed the tape by smashing and throwing it in the garbage.

Ten is the time our man ever stole anything. His sister was practicing for a dance competition in Sioux Falls and our man tagged along with his mom to be a supporter. In the afternoon in the sliver of downtime before the evening performance, our man wandered next door to the cultural bastion in Sioux Falls besides the Pomp Room, Zandbroz Variety. There, he browsed the books, not looking for serious fiction—that kind of thing would never interest him—but for the books on positions and naked everything. For a few minutes our man browsed in the sex and relationships section, being careful not to be seen, and if anyone did walk by he'd turn around and pretend to be checking the opposite row of books, but just as soon our man would turn again and dig deeply and read and look as fast as he could, as if trying to teach his brain to do more than it ever had or would again, to imprint all the beautiful forms and direct talk of how to give the best "blow job." That is, until he came upon one of the books. It was slim, hardly thicker than a couple of packs of baseball cards. Our man had found the most perfect thing. So frank in its teachings of sexual positions, which is what intrigued our man the most. The participants were all placed against muted white backgrounds, as if the models made love in the clouds, with intimate showcasing of their hair and real breasts. Oh, to imagine, as our man did, what it would be like to one day be their husband. He would need to study these positions so he could fully master them, if by pantomiming, before that happened. He did not want to be a novice. Our man put the book back and did a quick stroll around the store, feigning interest as he passed the hippie trinkets and cat jewelry and books on politics, all the while his mind racing with the thought of stealing. Buying? Not possible. His mom would find out, somehow. The cashier would take our man by the ear and right to her. Right then, the amazing thought reached his mind once more: he could just take it. It was small enough to put down his pants and walk out. Our man purposefully wandered back to it, and after a few hesitant touches and furtive looks, his heart beating hard enough that his shirt seemed to rustle, he stuffed it down his pants, just like he'd planned seconds before, then walked out of the store and miraculously caused no alarms. Our man could barely breathe as he looked back and no one was coming after him. He had it. He actually possessed it. Back at the theater, he hid the precious tome in a box of golf balls he bought that day. That little book was the most treasured thing our man would ever own.

⊰∞⊱

After the time of solitude, our man found himself in York, Nebraska. He got a hotel room, booted up his computer with a slight twinge of nervousness, and readied himself for the best of things. Lying on the made bed after a hot shower, completely naked, he read the first review.

"Where do I begin. Well, this app is total garbage. It's cool it's free, I guess, though I don't understand how the person who made it intends on making any money. What is this thing supposed to do? After a day I am confused and annoyed. Honestly, and I am not exaggerating here, the thing will ding at you once every damn hour with some instruction on how to be happy, and most are really stupid like 'Hug a stranger' and shit like that. I liked the layout, and again it was free, but I would not recommend this app to anyone looking for true happiness, like the app advertises. They won't find it here."

The next comment said, "Dumb," and the third one started with, "I made 100 dollars an hour working from home…"

Three comments. The total number of downloads? Thirty-six, and according to the analytics the numbers had precipitously dropped after the second day online. The day before, there had been no downloads. So far that day, again, none.

For several months our man had not drank or looked at the internet. At that moment he wanted to fill a bathtub with whiskey and swim in it, and to watch videos of young women with full thick hair and hairy crotches engaged in all sorts of acts their parents would have raised them not to do. Our man threw his phone across the room and it made a sick cracking sound. He put on the shirt and shorts he had not changed in weeks and sauntered to his car. Punching the radio left his knuckles bloody, and he started to drive. In the liquor store our man did not acknowledge the worker, who asked if everything was all right. After that our man drove on the highway, taking swigs of whiskey and not caring about the police. He stopped at a giant warehouse, its insides overwhelmed with flesh and the smell of rubber and human sweat. Our man went straight to the amateur videos and bought those he thought seemed the most real, with the budding breasts and unsullied crotches, then walked mutely to the counter, passing single men, those who were soon to be high on cocaine with a prostitute and in the morning would drive large loads of packaged food to Nevada or Missouri. After the purchase, our man made a beeline back to his car. He threw the black plastic with the videos onto the passenger seat and reversed out with one hand, swirling up the gravel and dirt. After squealing out on the main road, he very nearly caused an accident by pulling right in front of a semi. The semi fishtailed, causing its load to swerve into the other lane, narrowly avoiding a minivan going the opposite direction. Straight back to the hotel room, our man put the DVDs in and watched as he drank and masturbated.

At about the same time in the parking lot of the hotel, a family of four pulled up in their van after a close call a few miles back. Their plan was to go to Minnesota for the Mall of America. They'd also be visiting family and seeing a Twins game. Mom carried one of her children in her arms. Dad held the hand of the other. That night before bed, they hugged and kissed their little ones more sweetly, appreciating more sincerely their generous lot.

The next morning in the midst of sorrow and an extreme hangover, head a cloud and heart beating fast, our man thought of the one person who gave hope. She had shown interest by wearing star-spangled underwear. Her body soft, and her apartment full of hedonistic pleasure. Our man began to roll around on the ground, trying to gain his bearings as early-morning light wormed its way through the heavy curtains. The air conditioning on full blast, he pulled down the tucked-in comforter from the bed.

Why did he ever leave in the first place? Why did he try to do better than Aurora? Our man became consumed with regret on the floor of the budget hotel room. Perhaps, he dared to think, he had missed one of her calls. Who knew, with the spotty service in the areas he traveled. Perhaps she sat in underwear playing video games, smoking weed, every so often putting down the controller to go to the kitchen for a snack, not thinking about how much of her ass showed while eating standing up. Her weight on one leg, absently dreaming of what could have been between her and that odd but sweet guy with the ad for cleaning apartments with his tongue.

"My god," our man imagined her thinking. "He gave the best sex in years."

Her hips swayed when she walked away to another room to get more marijuana, and it seemed to our man a satisfied walk, full of tender lust for the next time. Our man peeled himself off the ground and clumsily hit a few buttons to wake his computer. It turned back on to loud peals of orgasm, and he immediately shut that window down and opened another to call Aurora. Using this service, he could call for free. That had been a good idea.

"A useful one," our man chided himself. "What kind of frivolous shit is happiness? Or video games even. They're at least full of useful programs and design and animation that take work and provide content that people will pay money for. Why can't I come up with something that people want?"

The thought had germinated in our man for years and now sprouted mushroom spores over his brain. The heavy drinking didn't help, moving from town to town, never going to graduate school or making tactical decisions online. Maybe, he faintly recalled thinking before going to Mountain View, he could find someone with a bit less around the middle, a slightly cuter face, and thicker hair.

Who was he to talk? God had blessed Aurora with sensual mouth, and the fat around her hips made her womanly. Hardly any hair remained on the top of our man's head; how could he demand Aurora carry all the water? Those thoughts of better ones had to be the deranged ravings of a power-blind programmer. Now, our man knew, he could settle in the Midwest, lose weight, go back to school, do his best to get a decent job, then work himself up to the best man possible for Aurora, who would surely make him happy every morning and night for the rest of his life.

Nervously, our man clicked on the number and the computer began to mimic the noise one used to hear when a call needed to be supported by huge wooden posts over long stretches of ditches across the country. He prayed for Aurora to pick up. What a relief it would be to hear her voice. He yearned for it, even if his yearning had always been his greatest sin. The computer continued to make the sound of a ring and no human picked up. Our man composed himself. He gave the most cordial message he could muster.

"Hi Aurora. So, yeah, kinda fell off the map there. Where did I go? What did I do? All very good questions we're thinking right now, and I'd like to answer them for you. I suggest we go through them over dinner. I know a place in Bayview that has the best pho, then we'll go down the street to the Palm and have a whiskey and touch butts. I mean, not each other's butts, our own butts, and the people we meet, those butts, though I guess we could also touch each other's butts, because I think we got some good ones, Aurora,

I do. Anyway, I'm rambling about butts again. I should stop while I am way behind. Okay. Look forward to hearing from you. By the way, my number is…"

And our man proceeded to reiterate his number, as if Aurora didn't have it, then clicked a button to hang up the phone and started to wait. He picked up the hotel room's television remote from the bureau, but before he could even get past the general welcome screen that advertises for the premium channels, he received a text.

"Hey," Aurora wrote. "Sorry to hear about you falling off the map. Things have been really busy for me lately. I hope you make it back safely, from wherever you've been, and I hope you're doing great, but I don't think I see us hanging again. Good luck in the future!"

He lay there on the hotel bed, letting the stillness envelope him. The silence of the muted figures on the television. Cool air shooting out of the rumbling air conditioner. Smoothness of the cheap comforter. The message continued to sting. So much, our man slithered off the bed, positioned himself on the floor, and reared back his head and slammed it against the dresser. Smashing it as hard as he could, over and over again until blood ran down his face. When he could no longer muster the strength, he passed out. And there he lay, until the maid service found him.

HOW I BECAME GOD

The light that took me came as dim flashbulbs, swinging back and forth, then it coalesced into a luminous glow. The sky became a searchlight, and I shielded my eyes. When it became night once more, I found myself in Minneapolis, where I lived before I moved in with the psychiatrist.

Unremarkably I lived there, as I have lived everywhere. Never did I leave a place imprinted with my memory. No trophies or keys to the city have been given to me. No riots incited because of something I said or revolutions started because of what I wrote. No statues of my body erected. No wings of hospitals named in my honor. I never owned land or a home or livestock to slaughter and feed a growing family. I moved from place to place while drinking and complaining to others of my troubles. My existence could be summed up as a series of banking movements within my head made in an attempt to commandeer an infinite, uncontrollable space. I never succeeded, so I evolved into a mass of seconds and minutes, then hours and days and years, of someone who worried over each consequence before ever deciding on anything.

Back to the light that took me to the city I lived in before I lived with the psychiatrist, in Minneapolis, and as I landed I thought of her lithe body and soft face. The first time she said she it we were talking on the phone in our bordering states.

"Yes," she said, "I love you."

But I did not say it back. I wanted to tell her in person. I did not want her to think I was only saying it because she did.

Back once more to the light. It brought me to the living room of a house in the suburbs of Minneapolis where I once lived. Brenna is there playing video games on the couch. A recent college graduate, she has eyes like a fish's bulging out of her face. She is taller than I, and I am six feet tall. The room smells like her, the remains of weed and light perfume. The year is 2011, though I am not sure of that. Time is fluid, and I am suckling like a newborn on the teat of a tall blonde hammer thrower.

"So that's my boob?" she says, and he looks up from the devoted suction of her breast.

How embarrassing to see a man so prostrate. High on drugs and twenty-three and taller than most, I watch as she plays the video game and he kisses her. When she encounters a townsperson in the Camelot village—the kind where they wear fur skins and sell pounds of rabbit or raw iron ingot—she slices without remorse but says, "Oh God, what am I doing. Jesus, this is terrible," right as she keeps on, smirking as she cuts them down. He laughs too, then goes back to her breasts.

"Sit up like a man," I shout now, but he cannot hear. "If she is looking for someone to get high and play video games and touch she will call one of the friends she has for that." My face is now red with exhaustion.

The first time he saw her, Brenna wore a gas mask, though she would never survive in a war. The smoke dissipated from her peach-colored cheeks and plates for eyes, yet even as she exhaled, she did not look up through her screen. Yet I held on to hope. That first night, after meeting through the dating website, we talked for an hour, and by the end of the next week I had fallen. Brenna would come over to the suburbs and get high and play video games and we would laugh and I'd take off one of her ratty rock-band t-shirts and we'd do everything. Now I am dead or a ghost or a god as I watch myself suckling on Brenna's breasts like a newborn kitten on its mother.

"Get up," I shout. "What are you going to do, be her servant for the rest of time?" But neither of them hear.

Below me now, the floor of the house in the suburbs in Minneapolis has turned to glass. Saltwater crashes up into the foundation, and I see him put his head on her stomach as she takes another hit and keeps playing the video game. He begins to taste her, and she puts up a good theater for him. For their finish minutes later, he spills it all between her legs. I watch as he walks out of the living room, happy and accomplished, though he has done nothing. Brenna waits for him to get back from the kitchen with the paper towels. Immobilized as if she has been shocked with a Taser, she does not move, not wanting any of it to fall into her. She rolls her eyes, reaching her long arm to the coffee table to retrieve her phone. Now as I could not before, I see the text she sends, written in the waves below me.

"Where are you?" she writes. "I'm coming over soon. Also, I hate online dating."

Gallons of cold sea fill my stomach as a beast approaches. Thousands upon thousands of creatures are being swallowed up and spit out by its current. If I can just get to the surface, land could be nearby. I swim with everything I have to where the light is dancing and reflecting. For second, peace, like the thing took another route. I find the surface, and just as I do a whale the size of a state jumps out of the water. Its arc of flight descends on me, and I can do nothing but peer up into its gaping mouth, dripping down animal flesh and salt water. Inside now, and it is better here. Unlike Jonah before, the whale and I come to an agreement.

"You can stay as long as you like," the whale says. "Also I wanted to tell you. I know you think everything always ends with people eating each other alive, but it doesn't have to. Not always." Right as he finishes part of his tongue turns into a stairway, leading me up to the blowhole, and as I walk up the stairs I think about that. I imagine the psychiatrist on the couch, drinking espresso and acclimating herself to her day. Later, us making soup and watching a movie as she lies on top of me like a lovely paperweight. I always said I wanted to be punished for the things I did wrong. I don't want that anymore.

On top of the whale, I see for miles in every direction. The sun is bright and the beast slippery, so I slide. I punch at the bumps and parasites; they splatter as I whoosh down. At the bottom, shaking off the water, I turn and wave to the whale, and its mass is blotting out the sun. A simple thunderous clap of its tail, and it swims hundreds of miles away. The water it displaces falls like light snow as I step through the door of a wooden backyard fence, to green grass and a back porch where there is grilling.

Two daters have sat down to eat the food and drink the drinks that he, who was once me, prepared. I listen to the conversations and to how he forces something that is not there. Most of those he meets that summer while online dating are friendly and attractive, and their ghosts listen above their bodies. One of the ghosts comes over and offers me a cloud beer. I decline, and she floats back. The rest of the spirits just hover while waiting for their night to end. They cannot understand, as I cannot now, why their bodies have come. We both wonder why strangers try and coerce such a thing as ungraspable as "love." The ghosts seem frustrated with themselves for even agreeing to the date in the first place. One body in particular has been fooled into meeting someone who was not, as her previous lover in France, an Australian model with "actually, kind of like a perfect face." But she tells him, who was once me, on a back porch in the suburbs of Minneapolis, that she does not like the model anymore, though we can tell—him, me, her ghost, her body—that she is lying. Earlier in the night, talk of fireworks.

"We'll shoot them off when it's dark," she said with a flower in her hair, but she left before the sun went down. Nothing lit the dark except the streetlights.

I watch as they have their goodbye. He is giving her—a Midwestern girl with a pert backside and freckles—a cautious hug. This is the last time they will see each other, that is clear to everyone in the universe but my body. He believes they will go on another date, all the way up until a week later when she texts to say she has not been able to respond to the messages he sent because her "phone battery has been acting up." Her ghost flips me off as they leave, for later when he alludes to her body being a liar about the phone.

Now she has driven away, and I follow what one would technically call a man back inside a house in the Minneapolis suburbs. By age and physical development, it's what he is. He closes the front door, and I think of what the whale said, that not everything has to end like it does, all these sad hearts breaking. The one with the flower in her hair ate him alive, and I understand why. I think I do get it now. I was not a man. I was a pus-filled sack of bald weakness. A decaying sack of meat. The one with the flower in her hair ate a tub of decomposing jelly, and there is no crime in that. I should have not pressed for justice when there was none to be given.

Wandering through the house then into the backyard, strolling past the smoky residue of the meal—bits of ketchup on the varnished wood, gnawed pieces of grilled asparagus with butter and salt—I find myself now in a forest where my sister and I played near the house where we grew up. We carved out a fort called Calypso, named after the John Denver song, and defended it from intruders by standing for goodness and right. I find the trees comforting, and the rhythm of my steps hypnotic. I did not notice the bear rising like one of the trees.

First was the smell. Then, the breathing. saliva falling in buckets on my head. I stop, but do not dare look. It must be so big it could eat me like a pea. I get on my knees, then fall flat on the ground as the beast rears back on its hind legs. It roars, and the ground shakes. My head will split, I'm sure, but just before my brain leaks the sound stops, and the bear takes one giant step over me, then another, and another, stamping down the trees in its path. That makes it easy to track. Miles later, I come upon its cave where I find her, as massive as a skyscraper, sleeping with her cub. We are in the crook of our mother's arm. A bed of warm fur. I nestle in to rest and I begin to dream.

I wake alone. The cave has become the locker room in the gym of my high school on the day when a boy in my class takes a shampoo bottle and rams it inside another classmate. I watch as Tim falls to the floor of the shower. Laughing and snickering, the boys in my class repeat as they get dressed that they just cannot "fucking believe" what happened, that he would actually "lose his shit" like that. Everyone goes to the next class except Tim and I. His wet brown hair straying every direction, his wiry frame hunched over, Tim does not look at me. He will be a mechanic and compete in sprint car races, marry and have three children. I saw naked breasts for the first time at his parents' house from a taped copy of *Bikini Carwash Company*.

"Sorry," I say, sure he cannot see me or hear me. "I should have done something."

But to my surprise, Tim looks up. He is staring through me.

"You're a coward, like me." Tim finishes tying the laces of his shoes. "No matter how many lifetimes you're given, you won't say or do anything. And that's fine, I'll grow up and do what I love, have a wife and children, and they'll never know about any of this. But if I can be a man and forget things, things harder than what you went through, why can't you? Why do you live the same events over and over, going back and forth through time? For what? The psychiatrist loves you. You love her. What more do you want?"

Then Tim got up and left me alone in the locker room. For how long I stayed there, I do not know.

The school melts into a candle I hold in my hand. Its ash is like sulfur, body odor and chalk. Flesh falling from my bones, I will be a skeleton soon. After that, just dust. As particles of fluff, I am free to float the earth. A wisp bobbing over mountains, over fields of crops, to the bottom of chasms where everything is silent and heavy. Down there, I am eaten by a worm who is then eaten by a fish who is eaten by a bird who gave birth to a baby bird who has become me, and I am glad. Always I have wanted to be a baby bird. Life as a baby bird, I once imagined, would be so simple. To have someone lie on top of you and ensure your warmth and shoot food down your mouth; that's all. You do not even need to chew. The only expectation is to fly, and that I learn more quickly than my baby bird brothers and sisters. I try not to laugh at their attempts, remembering where I have been. I want my brothers and sisters to succeed and have their best attempts applauded, not sneered at. I excel so much my bird mother wants me to show the others how to fly.

"Cheep-cheep," she says, but I am too far away from the nest. My family is far behind. I keep flying toward the horizon.

Above a mountain in the clouds. Peaks in the thin air, and I see down below one road precariously swerving its way through it all. Who would construct that path? Who would choose to walk it? I see him who was me. That's who would do it. At that point he is working at a bookstore in his thirties, balding and gaining weight, an adult mess of anxieties and fear and guilt, yet he climbs. From my vantage point it seems a better option would be to fall one way or the other. Looking at what's ahead and seeing what he's equipped with, there is no way he will make it. Just evaporate into the clouds, bud.

Still he goes up the mountain, to a castle where he and a dark-haired woman eat soup on their first online date. He has become a mouse, and she is a python. Just squeaks are his words, diminishing and constricting in her coil as he prattles on about what he thinks he knows about this author or what that story in *Tin House* meant, or even the tales of when he attended his state land-grant college and fell in love with Jesus, all of his wasted breath helps tighten her grip as she hisses her beginnings in Manhattan, she wrote for the *Times* and would be graduating soon with her MFA from the University of Minnesota. They hug at the end, he thinks, but from the sky above I see the snake retract its jaw and swallow the mouse, making what looks like a Goya.

He emerges from the snake's bowels as jangling bones with hair in strange places, staggering but going up, desperate to reach a castle with spires and icy blue clouds floating above a moat. I know who'll be there, another online date. He believes it is his birthright to accompany her as her king. Not to rule, but to satisfy when she calls and fulfill her needs. It was scrawled upon his soul, to find The One in the blinding white coldness. He must quell its burning. The searing eats him alive. He comes upon the second queen in her study, her curly hair taking up the room. I fly above, hearing the screams. Of pleasure first, as they enjoy what there is to enjoy, then of terror as she rips him limb from limb. Using his bones as sticks, his head as a brush and his blood as paint, she smears him on a canvas with the colors of others she has been with and liked more, those with higher-paying jobs who she could take home to her family in Connecticut whose sons and daughters study abroad for a semester. Her work finished, he leaves with colors dripping off his body. Walking feebly, his legs giving out every few steps. I need to at least try to get him to stop. I perch on his shoulder and tell him what is waiting for him at the next castle, but my words come out as squawking and he bats me off his shoulder.

I fly above, close enough to see his bloody footsteps. They kept him awake at night dreaming of someone who has no thought of him. Forward, though, forward, his belief is unwavering, and so it does not surprise me to see, when he arrives at the last gate, that his heart has the right password. The huge wooden door goes up chain by chain, each link as big as a car. How happy he is to be let in, so happy he is blind to the sign pointing to the graveyard where other adventurers are buried in the garden out back, each with a head-stone showing the code that also granted them entrance. It does not matter what their heart said, only how weak it made them to keep on writing so many different codes. A mush, they could fit anyone.

A pile of malleable liquids arrives in the last queen's chamber, sliming its way across the marble floor toward her ornate throne like a slug. I soar along the glass windows over a canyon. Though even as slime, he believes he is as strong and as good as any other she has entertained. Just barely I can hear their conversation, the wind howling and tilting my path. She picks him up and kisses him, causing a drool of fluids to flow down her majestic chin. After her amorous display is done, she says to the curtain of sludge, "This is getting to be too much, too soon."

"Bring me a towel," she demands, and in a flash a servant is there with a fresh cloth folded over his arm. Without ceremony, she wipes off the trail then gives the soiled rag back to the servant, who discards it in a bin. The bin leads to the furnace, and as I fly away ashamed I pass through a billow of the acrid, black smoke.

Back on the ground, typing these words, I am now free to write the story I have always wanted to write. In this story I possess a full head of hair and a package just a little too big. Every pair of jeans I try on fits me well. Nothing is too tight around the thighs. I am with the psychiatrist, and everything is good. We make pho and go to the movies whenever we like. My love is so much she can only take fractions of it. My job is writing novels. A publisher in New

York City pays me. I fly in planes to London and Paris to talk about my work. Everything I say is retweeted.

The parchment vanishes, and I lose the pen. I am not a bird but a passenger behind him. This is his first plane ride. The destination is in Alabama. Only about half of the seats are occupied. I am a row behind where he sits alone looking out the window with his headphones on. I can touch his wrist and feel blood pumping like a heartbeat from God. This is the portrait of a young man venturing to start a Christ-like courtship. How long he has yearned for this. Stavesacre plays in his ears as he becomes more sure this trip has been willed by Elohim. Transmissions are sent, radio waves between him and God. He prays for what will happen in Alabama with a woman named Katherine. I see now God sending down static in return, but still he prays, his messages going up like a string of notes. If arranged on a score, they would clang out of tune.

I am a plant Katherine waits behind. For the last month she has spent much of her time, outside of the organic grocery store her family runs, on the phone with a South Dakotan she met on MySpace. Katherine has told him, in the kind of detail he loves but also hates because it is a sin, of the blow jobs she has given, of how the best time to have sex is in the afternoon, and of the time she didn't really do it with a man in Colorado because he only went in "once or twice" and also the other times she used his hand inside her in conjunction with the tip of his penis rubbing her clitoris. She said she loved a man for a long time who was very well equipped but she broke up with him. He sold drugs and Katherine had become a believer in Christ.

Katherine is hiding, and I can tell, by the way she braces my pot, she hopes the one coming down the wide hallway in the airport—light spilling through where outside the planes land on the tarmac—will be the man she is with for all time, that he will be everything her pastor preached a man of God should be. Her brown hair smells like my flowers.

Will he be as smart? she wonders. Still as sweet but manly too? Capable of one day finding a good job in creative marketing at her nationally known nondenominational church? She peeks out, and there he is, smiling as he strides toward us. I can tell by his face, but mostly because I was him, he cannot believe how attractive she is. They hug, then walk away holding hands.

I go to her place passing through the ground like a mole, and for the next days pay close attention to her thoughts. Katherine cannot stop thinking about the dark circles under his eyes, how they are more pronounced than she would have imagined her husband's to be, and his forehead is dry. It's the facial wash he used to remedy a recent bad patch of acne, he said. More than that, she worries his penis is not as she once hoped her husband's penis would be, and there is the unforgivable sin of him in her bed. It's not what a spiritual leader would do, she thinks as she takes Jeffrey down to her cave of a bedroom once more, and she comes up for air with wiry hairs in her mouth. She asks if he has ever shaved down there.

"Should I?" Jeffrey responds. The things he will have to learn, how they mount, though the most troubling problem of all, what courses through Katherine's head like a beating tell tale heart from Christ, is the problem of this guy not being able to keep himself ready. Even as Jeffrey gazes at her large breasts and Katherine wears her black see-through boy shorts, even after that, she knows it will never be enough. God did not will this to be so. It was written in His book before any star was made.

I walk up Katherine's two stairs, through the room she called an apartment and out the front door of the multi-unit home in the gay gentrified area of Birmingham. Out into the heat, through the segregated neighborhoods, I board the plane without Jeffrey. He has a lot to go through, and I am already tired of it. I'd like to be alone.

Landing in the middle of a pasture in northern Minnesota, close to the farm where Anne grew up. I trek down to a creek where I find her swimming nude. The sun wanes, and the field turns orange. The early evening is halcyon. Her body is the model for some pastoral cinema. When they knew each other in Seattle, to him every day was idyllic. He saw her, then through an even more baffling set of events, began seeing others as well. Even in my state of celestial ghostliness, I cannot understand why. He could have been with a beautiful hippie with a good head on her shoulders who laughed well and danced to Miley Cyrus songs after a few beers. She grew up on a farm and worked outdoors building houses. She visited Spain and kissed better than anyone he kissed. She would have doted on him for all time, if he had allowed it. She is not ashamed. Her breasts are small and her torso is long. She gathers a towel and I go to where she is drying her hair. She rests her ass, tan and athletic, against a giant rock.

"What are you doing?" she asks, working her curls dry. "You shouldn't be here."

"Anne, I don't know how I got here. Could we talk?"

"Talk about what?" Anne asks. Sunning herself on the rock, her body a golden example.

"Us, I think."

"There's no us, pal."

A surge knocks me over. "But do you remember," I say from the ground. "Do you remember when I came over while you took a bath. I got burritos, and when I got back you'd left your door open and I walked in and you wore a towel but you let it drop. Or what about when we watched that scary movie and you hid your face in my chest. Or when I thought we were done but then you got up and took the candle from my desk but didn't say a word and told me to follow you. We showered in the candle-lit darkness. I'm so sorry, Anne." I plead like a child to show my remorse. I eat the brown sand.

"Buddy. Get up." She does not want to enable my groveling.

"Am I supposed to be punished?" Muddy soil falls from my mouth.

"We don't meet people at the wrong time," Anne says, wrapping her towel around herself. "We just meet the wrong people."

Her words pound me into the ground, to where they dig for oil and minerals, where it smells like blackness. "Please," I shout, eating the earth. "I thought about you for years."

Anne moves away from her rock and the soil collapses around me.

"No," I say, muffled, though my words have stopped mattering. It gets colder, until it all of a sudden becomes very hot.

The earth opens and I fall into a boat. A man oars me to the gates. His face is cloaked.

"Don't know what you did wrong," he says gently. "But I'm sorry for where you're going. Might be saying too much, but I never understood why He destines some for this place and others for up there. I suppose be glad you're not that guy."

On the banks a man is hanging from a tree, wildly attempting to free himself from a noose. My lips are sewn shut, so I don't say a thing. Down below are rivers like waterfalls, descending like Escher. Soon enough, the man oaring the boat tells me to get out. I jump in the black water and begin to drown, dying hundreds of times. Swimming madly each time I wake up, I use the bars of the gate to help me go lower, to find they descend forever. Back at the surface, I shake at them violently.

"You shouldn't do that," I hear the man say.

Later, I somehow make it to the shore. Emerging from the water, the muck falls off me in roaches. There is no one around. It seems more like heaven should be, as if anyone is welcome, but I know innately that can't be true. Hell is not a free zone where you can come and go as you please. It is a one-way street. Once you pass through the membrane—on the boat ride, maybe when we saw Judas—there is no returning.

I am taken on an assembly line to a solitary building at the end of a vast prairie. The sky is gray above a shack at the edge of a lake and behind it is a chasm. The cabin is worn-down, like the vacation home of a middle school gym teacher who wanted somewhere to fish on the weekends after retirement. Inside, an immaculate, futuristic space, with not a piece of dust. It gleams all chrome, with a silver desk in the middle. A woman appears wearing a pressed gray suit.

"Sit down," she says, and I obey without really doing anything. Her face is millions of other faces superimposed on top of each other, like the eventuality of human evolution. I think she is stunning, achingly so.

"What are you doing here?" she asks like a high school principal asks a student who has misbehaved.

"I don't know. I was on this plane, but before that I was just at home with my wife. We were having dinner, then I started floating in space and there were these lights. I was meeting people I'd known before. Then I was writing this book. And..."

"Covetousness. Lust. Idleness," the woman says. "These are your sins."

"I've always tried to do my best," I say, and that maks her face change into the face of a goat, and I begin to burn.

"You are guilty," she says, filling up the whole room. "You are guilty of coming on a woman but not saying hello to her on the street when you saw her the next winter. You are guilty of pretending others did not exist. You are guilty of using, lying, making others feel like they are unwelcome. You are guilty of not using the cross-walk when you should have and that caused many deaths. Merging too soon on the highway and killing innocent people by not looking in your rearview mirror enough, you did all these things. You are bound to hell eternally. Now leave."

Before I can go anywhere, the woman vanishes and the room is no longer perfect. Now it is like the one in my mind, with fishing rods and reels, a fireplace and an aging hound dog, a kitchen littered with beer in cans and Spam on paper plates. I walk to the back door and pray one last time for old time's sake. Hearing nothing, I go forward into the emptiness.

A pierced man is standing over me, saying, "Rise now" as he shakes my shoulder. The rousing opens my eyes. I try to speak.

"Quiet now," he says, "rest. That was a long trip."

I notice my skin is charred blackness. I want to believe the man above me. For years I was down in hell, a place of constant reminders of every wrong step taken in life.

"Thank you," I say, but he disappears like so many doves.

I see a hot rod nearby, so why not, I get in and peel out. A trail leads me to the country and to Highway 81 that goes through Johnny Carson's hometown of Norfolk, Nebraska. I take it until hooking up with Interstate 80, driving to an exit for a small town. The one

God chose for me to marry will be there. With only about ten miles to go, Jesus shows up in my passenger seat, asking if He can pick the music. I say yes, and we listen to Jars of Clay's first album. "Love Song for a Savior" plays.

"Great track," Jesus says as He taps His feet and hums along perfectly, every part of the song—drums, guitar, vocals—coming out of His mouth at once. I want to talk, so Jesus stops singing and turns down the music with His mind.

"What is it?" He asks.

"Right, but you already know, don't you?"

"Yes, Lamb, but what kind of conversation can we have if you don't tell me?"

I keep my hands on the wheel even though I know He would steer us if I let go. "I just want to know if I'm going down this path for some specific reason or if this is supposed to be more torture? I'm wondering if maybe I'm still in hell but don't know it?"

"Your passion, Jeffrey, I have always admired."

That's all Jesus says before He turns Jars of Clay back on without moving a muscle. I want to add, "That wasn't much of a conversation," but I know He can hear what I think. Instead, I try to think of nothing, which is more difficult than anything.

We are headed to where I first worked after college. It's the weekend during the summer in Nebraska, and the rest of the houseparents and children from the orphanage are waterskiing at the lake.

After parking my car on a gravel driveway, Jesus floats away to heaven and I am left to wander the campus alone. Nothing has changed. The air is hints of hog farming and freshly cut grass, chlorine from the city pool. The light of this village is clarion, with real stars just above the field, burning blue. I take steps in the direction of the off-duty house where I lived with two other houseparents, first in the kitchen with carpet on the floor, past the old dining room with the chandelier and living room no one used, its wood floors and original moldings, then an office with a bay window that is like the living room of a famous play-wright. Going downstairs I walk on the shag carpet, so smooth that once I slipped while carrying my basket of laundry down the steps and my whole body went into the air. I came down so hard I thought I cracked my tailbone. Down to the basement where I once played *Halo* with Seth and Casey, to Casey's room, with his closet with boxes and boxes of Jordans worth thou-sands of dollars, then back out to my communal space where I kept my record player and books on theology and dating and the poster on the concrete foundational wall of a tree from the liner notes of a Danielson Famile album, and a loveseat no one ever sat in, and my desk where I wrote in my journal about Megan for over a year. There's a bathroom with the fan always on to suck up the rank humidity from the carpet. Finally to my small room, the one the headmaster of the orphanage told me to live in when I arrived. I thought it was strange but did not complain. It seemed that room would be enough, just a single bed with a blue blanket and my alarm clock and Bible. To watch the sun filter in and pray for my wife, a long-haired volleyball player from Iowa. She is too attractive to be here working at the group home, I thought from the start, but also believed God placed us there so we could have a funny story to tell new church members---at the church we routinely attended in Iowa City, I imagined---when they asked where we met.

"Yeah," I'd tell them, in my tailored navy suit coat and crisp button-down and ironed jeans and brown dress shoes, "it's crazy. We were working at this group home in Nebraska, and she was visiting the first time we met, and I remember thinking there's no way she's coming back to work here. Just no way."

"Then I did," she'd say with a ho-hum swing of her arm.

"Then you did," I'd repeat, and we'd have a kiss, modest enough for God's house but intense enough to make couples jealous. They'd see her, a onetime collegiate volleyball player with long black hair like a stallion, and me with all my hair, as she would have relieved my stress, and a job as a spiritual advisor for our nondenominational church. Her job was at home where she looked after our two girls, Hazel and Claire.

Hazel and Claire never came into this world, and I can uncover why, if I hurry. Megan is arriving with the teens soon. I run to her off-duty house they called Green House at the end of a dirt alley next to the paved county road at the end of town. Someone's grandma lived there once, its white rock as a perimeter, garage door with windows, the puke-green overhang. The stale-smelling entryway is for shoes and potted plants and the wooden door has panes of opaque glass. There is a piano in the living room. Only a few times did I go there, down in Rebecca's room with its green-painted walls. We listened to Furthermore's *She and I* while Rebecca— the other new houseparent—told me about her boyfriend Asher in Indiana.

In Megan's room upstairs now is where I wanted to be before I even met her. Morning, and the sunlight streams effusively through her upstairs bedroom window. Once when we worked together I visited her, her eyes sleepy and her hair a fluffy mess, her big lips yawning from just rising. But he did not go all the way in. He guarded her heart. He waited years.

Everything is the same. The bed is made, now I am old enough to be her ancestor. Her diary is resting on her pillow like a mint. This book contains the Gnostic secrets. If given the choice, even in my steely days of resolve for Christ, I would have chosen Megan's book of secrets over His. Her diary contained the clues God did not want to give. So I pick it up it. Knowing I need to hustle, I skip over the parts about the growing pains of starting a new job after college.

Megan writes about how she misses her family. How the kids at the group home frighten her.

"How am I ever going to get them to listen to me?" I skip forward again, until I come across my name. "Jeff came over to Girls tonight. I wish he hadn't."

Right then the diary begins to burn, and now the bedroom crackles. They are driving back from waterskiing and they will blame me for this. I get down on my knees and crawl through the blaze to the kitchen. Hacking up the smoke, I take a chair and throw it hard against the sliding glass door but it barely cracks. Holding my breath, I try again. Nothing. I fling with my whole body, and at last the glass shatters. I sprint to a neighboring cornfield to hide from the police cars and fire trucks.

My onetime coworkers don't see me. I am obscured by the stalks. There is Jason and his voluptuous wife, Hope, with their adorable boys Micah and Seth. Candy, also with giant breasts, who would live with her mom in Omaha after the group home, is crying, and so is Rebecca, who always smelled like menstruating and who loved Asher, who came to visit once and smelled like raisins. Brian, the houseparent manager, who laughed with his whole body at the corny jokes he told, looks on in disbelief. At last, Megan, who would move back to Iowa and become a social worker and later marry the one who pressured her to have sex in college. She is not agog at the burning like the rest.

She is the only one looking into the cornfield. Her eyes are pointed straight at me.

∽∞∾

Years of running, and I catch my breath at the base of the Rocky Mountains. The blue rivers, brown terrain, white caps in the distance. Sunshine. Younger than before, I have not met Megan, so there is hope. This summer I will share God with others. He wants to be in love with them. Among a gleeful throng, so fresh-faced, just out of their first or second year of college, I am glad to be proclaiming the love of Christ. Many here this summer from across the country to spread the Good News will find a partner for life. I hope for the same as I say goodbye to my dad, who has taken his boy to Colorado. My dad has an inward faith. He never believed in trying to convince others of something they cannot be convinced of, still he loves his boy, and is at least glad his son is not living with someone before marriage, risking having a child he cannot afford. I think my dad is happy I'm going to college and am involved with a group that might supply me with a "good-looking woman" who comes equipped with an extended family who would not want to drink at the wedding. We say goodbye, and he leaves me to my choices.

Outside in the open area of the apartment complex in Fort Collins, I am talking with new friends and soon-to-be co-evangelists, all of us sure of what will happen to us when we die. We talk of where we go to school and what our majors are and how we are doing with the Lord. All the while I am getting vertigo, looking around for her. I want her to walk up and say hello. She does not, so I choose a bench and start a conversation with a balding student in an Iowa Hawkeyes t-shirt. He will find a wife that summer.

Jeffrey, the one this whole thing is about, goes about that summer alone. I see him get up and walk to work by himself. The other budding evangelists drive a car or hitch a ride with someone they want to make out with in the group, but he walks on the sidewalk along a busy street listening to music on a Discman to the same songs over and over. He is a better-looking version of himself, but the way he walks is so grim, like he has been through grueling wars. Every weekend, he shaves his head and calls out to God.

"Please," he prays in the shower, blood dripping down his forehead. "I want to live closer to you. Lord, please help me walk in your steps."

While dearly hoping, though trying not to think specifically, that one of the girls, especially the brown-skinned one from Hawaii, could be his wife. Every weekday that summer Jeffrey goes to work at a daycare for the children of the adults who run the national interdenominational evangelical Christian organization. Those well-groomed adults are in Colorado to learn how to become better at bringing young college students to the one and only savoir on earth. Jeffrey and the other proselytizing youth watch the children of those parents. During the day is Bible school with the kids and at night there are meetings and small groups where the guys get together and confess their sexual sins while the young ladies discuss what a Godly man will look like.

"David, Noah, and Jesus rolled into one," one says at a meeting I attend as a ghost. I remember her, a blonde from Florida who fervently believed in angels and demons living among us and had a gap between her front teeth.

On weekends Jeffrey goes to a nearby park and listens to the same album over and over, specifically a song called "Gold and Silver" by the band Stavesacre. As it plays he writes in his journal about what it means to live as a true follower of Christ. I stand over where he is lying on the grass near an abandoned baseball park. He thinks his head looks less bald when brown. As he listens to the music and soaks in the sun, Jeffrey prays to the creator of the universe for more courage to tell strangers about Jesus.

"Everyone has heard the story and made up their mind," is what I say, but it does not matter. He can't hear me, or maybe he already knows and he secretly thinks his innocence will help persuade someone to accept the Gospel. If he works hard enough, they might one day be in heaven together.

Summer goes along and one day I follow Jeffrey and the rest downtown. The cargo-shorted, gel-haired leader inspires the group with a speech first, and afterward lets them loose. Jeffrey manages to go off by himself, and I now find that more impressive than lonely, as the specific instructions were to have a partner. I know who he will approach too. He looks for a male, not a female, as he and the others had been told by the leader not to approach the opposite sex, even if I now see a group of more socially-advanced male missionaries approaching attractive young women. Up ahead, Jeffrey spots a man with a beaten-up backpack and pieces of large poster board resting against a potted plant. The man has a long beard, down almost to his waist. Closer now, the man smells like he has not showered in weeks.

With the booklet of four spiritual laws in his hand, Jeffrey can give hope. Maybe, Jeffrey thinks, the man will turn over a new leaf and get sober, find a job and rent an apartment, marry, have children, and one day become wealthy enough to name a wing of a hospital after the one who saved his life with the rejuvenating words of Christ. Jeffrey nears the man, pamphlet shaking in his hand, and as he extends his arm like a bayonet, he asks, "Sir, excuse me, do you know Christ?"

The man turns. "Christ?" he says. "I love Christ."

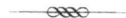

His name is Jerry, and he and I are at the gates of heaven now. We've been here for what seems like eons. Somewhere near the beginning, I told Jerry my theory about hell, how it seemed more welcoming than what's in front of us now, all golden and impressive but overpowering and cold. Jerry didn't find my theory all that interesting, or that appealing. He just keeps repeating, "While we were still sinners, He died for us."

This is Jerry's way of saying heaven was never meant for just anyone. One needs to recognize God's sacrifice, His Son's sacrifice, and the Spirit that lived within both of them, to be saved.

"Heaven has to be a special place, because it is a great place," is what I imagine Jerry would say, if he could say anything other than, "While we were still sinners, He died for us."

"Only those who earn the right can enter," he might add, even if I know on earth Jerry would have never used the word "earn." Anyway, we do not argue here, just outside heaven.

We stand and wait, with expanses of white clouds in all directions. In hell there was ground. In heaven there is only the not so reassuring air. I could plummet and never return, and that's maybe the point. We wait and wait. Jerry is an obedient dog. Every so often he looks up and shouts "Hallelujah." The rest of the time he sits with his legs crossed, bowing his head like Gandhi. On the other hand, I am restless and worried with no idea of what will happen.

Wandering off, I find the scenery never changes. The same golden rods going up forever and the same clouds. Exhausted, I put my head down, and it is so easy to sleep. Imagine the best bed. That bed is rocks and nails compared to sleeping in the clouds outside heaven. I blame the lavish comfort for what happened. I wake to a conversation in Aramaic, thinking I was dreaming, only to hear Jerry saying my name. My eyes shutter open, and I run, whirring the clouds, and I arrive back at the gate breathless.

"Thank you for joining us," Peter says when I get there. He looks the Peter in *Jesus Christ Superstar,* with a thick beard, a leather vest, no shirt, and pants laced with string. I can feel Jerry's disapproval.

"Sorry," I say. "I didn't know when we were meeting. I ran here as fast as I could."

"Be calm, son, time is no issue." And Peter is right about that. "The two of you are here today because God called you."

"Praise be," Jerry barks, his tongue hanging out.

"As you can see, I have my book," Peter says, tapping at the pages with a pen tipped in a glowing orb. "But that's just for show, of course." Then he throws the heavy book in the air and the pages turn into swans that swim-fly away.

"Thank you, Lord," Jerry says. I know Jerry will be let in and I know I will not be. He can see the ecstasy in front of him. It makes me infinitely jealous.

"Jeffrey," Peter says. "You have been selfish and full of anxieties and never happy during the one life God gave you. You have lied and been lazy and that is why you never got anything you ever wanted."

I do not argue. I stand there waiting to fall. I hope that part will be exhilarating, at least.

"And Jerry," Peter says, "you have been the same." A shocked second, and Jerry disappears. The terror in his puppy-dog eyes was the last thing I see.

How awful for Jerry, then in the next second I think, am I to meet God? This has been a long time coming. To be allowed in a place with all the people I loved the most and also the best-looking women I saw once on the street or at a party but never had a chance to talk to because I was too afraid? Curiously, Peter does nothing. He does not wave me forward or motion for someone to open the gates. He stands there. I tentatively step forward.

"So, do I go in now or...?"

Peter smiles, as if proud I would ask. "Oh Jeffrey. Heaven was made by the devil so he could trick people into feeling bad. You know it's not real like Colton said, right? Colton was a five-year-old boy brainwashed by his parents, but you're an adult who has seen the world. You know there's no place of eternal happiness, right?"

I have no time to answer. Dear Lord, I am falling again, leaving again for another place.

———— ∞ ————

A band of angels carries me. I think. They look like the angels from the stories, and I think they smell like angels, if angels have a smell. They also seem like the ones I dated online, with faces and breasts and backsides I recognize, now with wings and halos. Each has grown into a giant, though even in their menacing form they will not harm me. They are happy to have the task of taking me, or it could be they don't recognize who they are transporting. I did lose hair. I did gain weight.

We fly above the clouds and no one speaks. This goes on for a long time. We move above the world. Every so often I try to catch their eyes but they are committed to getting me wherever it is we are going. After a while we come up on a volcano, and just as I feel its warmth I realize they know who I am and I am dropped, like a baby by a stork. Looking up from my plummeting, I see they are waving at me. And giggling, covering their holy mouths.

I'd like this to end soon, all this falling. I miss the psychiatrist and the life we had begun to forge. It was more than I thought I could ever have after so many depressed years chasing after those who did not want to be caught, of moving to a city to flee the disappointment of failures in the previous city, of changing jobs, of not graduating with a degree that would allow me to get a worthwhile job, of not being good at math or handy with tools, of online dating, of hurting random people, of random people hurting me, of working at factories and warehouses, of part-time jobs college students would be ashamed of, of alienating the only ones who could have loved me, of years of being on the internet without gaining followers, of being jealous of people who were also on the internet who seemed to gain followers without trying, of wasting so much time. I found the psychiatrist by chance at a wedding in the South. She knew languages. She was trim and cried when she laughed. She cared for me.

Still I fall, and as I get closer to the volcano I shield my body from the sparks flying up. Reaching terminal velocity, I think about how I am not with a "twenty-two-year-old with a bubble butt"—as the psychiatrist joked about me wanting—and how that's a good thing. They only ever wreak havoc, the baby-powdered millennials with red hair and yoga pants and asses that make men weep pathetically. So I work my way back to my love. I fight and twist and contort my body, just missing the spurting magma, going straight for home. She is there; I know it, maybe searching for the remainders of what I left. Wrapping herself in our bed, crying herself to sleep.

I walk in the door and see someone else on the couch. The psychiatrist has made dinner for him, like she once did for me. They are relaxing with their meals and watching a movie. She puts her legs on him, rests her head on his shoulder in the same way. This man is a gentleman, not all rough-and-tumble like the ones she saw before me, the ones with penises the size of Coke cans. This man gets up in his dignified way even while wearing sweatpants, asks if she wants anything. She says "no, thank you, baby," and pulls herself into the blanket we once covered ourselves in, leans her head back in a kind of contented way. I want to ask where they met, but soon they are going to bed. So I leave, giving her what she deserves and did not get enough of with me: dignity, privacy, and respect.

—— ◦◦◦◦ ——

Travel to Barcelona and London and the South Pacific, to the Caribbean islands, Peru and Iceland. I now have the "agency," as they said in blogs before I left, but flying to these places, seeing their natural beauty, only makes me lonelier. I have to go where they will know me. I once fell away from my family, breaking off in disbelief---having sex without a wife, drinking to the point of getting drunk---and as the years went by we saw each other less and less. It was a great disappointment to my parents when I moved in with the psychiatrist before marriage, and an even greater disappointment when I went home to tell them she and I had broken up. They will welcome me now. I am their only son and brother. My two sisters with their husbands have children and they made lives like I never could. I go to see my mother and father. I have to show them how far I have come.

—— ◦◦◦◦ ——

After all this time I do not ring the doorbell. This is the small town on the plains where I grew up. I walk in through the garage, and there are the sedans, immaculate and shining. Cardboard boxes of crushed pop cans, assorted plastics, *Argus Leader*s and catalogs. Piled in a corner: hula hoops, a decaying red wagon my mother used to pull me and my sisters along our long gravel driveway in the country to get the mail, a scythe my father used for cutting weeds in the pasture, a blue tarp, a picnic table, decrepit sports equipment, cleaners for the cars. On the wall hooks are coveralls and hats. A host of mismatched and flattened worn shoes on mats on the ground. I gave those pairs to my father when done wearing them. He used them when he went out to see his cows. Cases of pop, cooling as if waiting for me to drink them if ever I came home. The door is heavy and opening and I am first overwhelmed by the smell, unnamable but so distinct I am twenty-one again, home for the summer. I sit at the island with a full head of hair, believing it is leaving me soon.

Time whirls ahead to the same kitchen—remolded with a wooden floor and new cabinets—and I am telling my parents I will be moving in with a woman. Over the age of thirty, mostly bald, and they are heartbroken that I would make such a decision before getting married. I am heartbroken too, seeing how they are. I imagine the conversations my father will have with his sisters, having to tell them his son is living with a woman to whom he is not even engaged. My mother hands me a tissue. I reach out to hug her but time spins forward and I stand watching myself in the future in this same home, helping my parents move out. I am bald and overweight and dependent on their money to live. I masturbate to pornography. I work at a job I hate. In my late forties, my mother still calls me handsome.

Times moves forward once more to where they are buried. To my mother's grave upon a hill overlooking the house her grandfather built along a river. Flowers for her are next to her father, who died when I was a teenager, and her mother, who died when she was. Then I am next to my father in the next town over, who is laid beside his father and his mother.

I look away and am carried back to the small town where my parents raised my sisters and me. No one is here. I go downstairs to where my father would watch the Cowboys game or an episode of *Bonanza* or *Andy Griffith*. I go up to their bedroom where my mother would be in bed after taking a bath, her hair wet and glasses on, reading a book or playing a word game on her tablet. No one is here, and now my knees buckle. I bury my head in their covers. This is the bed I slept in after I peed in my own as a timid boy. I did this until I was ten, settling between my mother and father. They did not say a thing. My mother cleaned the sheets in the morning. She kissed my forehead and told me I will always be loved.

Flying up and out of the house, above my hometown, higher and higher until all the towns of South Dakota are specks, then the cities of the United States, then the world. Always I was curious what kind of physical boundary set Earth apart from the blackness of space. What makes it look like the round bluish-green globe you see from the moon? A simple lesson in science could have taught me, if I would have understood.

In the stillness, swimming through the weightlessness. This is the kind of place where no problems can form. I swim and remember what it was like to swim as a boy. The feeling of going underwater where everything is muted. I could almost beat Josh Homer, the boy who would one day go on to win state in the 110-meter hurdles. We raced from one end of the pool and back again, and I could almost beat him. Swimming did not require the thumping of my clunky legs against the ground. It used the power within those trunks, and the smoothness of the strokes that I could create with my arms in accordance with the kicks of my legs. I prided myself on my swimming. I went to the pool almost every day, and there was baseball too. I was good at baseball. Unlike football or basketball, hardball did not require aggressiveness. Its internal competitiveness suited me. I could throw hard and teach my arm to fly the ball into the same spot on the catcher's mitt. Baseball and swimming, summer, youth. I was soft but not small.

I float in space and remember how as a boy I asked my father, while walking home from playing in the park, whether he thought I would make it as a Major League Baseball player. He took a moment, and even as a little boy I could tell he did not think I would. What my father wanted to be, I cannot say. I know he never wanted for me something far off and unattainable. He wanted a smooth road for his son, one that widened and became more agreeable with age. I could never find it. I instead found myself going up a steep, impassable road. From there, one couldn't even see the wide road. But that's all childhood stuff. I had good parents. I never want to apply for the childhood poignancy award.

Besides, I need to focus while swimming in space, looking for God. Or it could be that I am God. Peter, I know, wasn't being straight with me. Heaven would be like this, a never-ending bowl of peace.

If I could just find some people, we'd have a good time. We might spend the rest of forever exploring worlds, until we come across a world where women love bald men who have done nothing. In this land these ladies are in grad school for linguistics and have large backsides and are good at jump rope and laugh at stupid jokes. I look for that world as I swim through the universe. Past solar systems, I approach stars and hold their power in my hands. Simply brush by and replace their matter as casually as one returns a billiard ball to its felt. I find perfection in untouched centuries.

Keep swimming. Up and down, to the left and to the right, wondering what down and up and left and right even mean anymore. I was never any good at that, knowing where I was going. I could not clear-headedly solve equations in college calculus or high school algebra before that, or even elementary word problems before that. As a boy, I had special time in the resource room with the slow kids, learning how to multiply and divide. I went to a special room for my speech as well. A young woman came from Sioux Falls and drilled me with flashcards and I sounded out the words painstakingly, trying to rid myself of my lisp.

What am I talking about? What does any of that matter? I have to find God. He could sort all this out.

God could go inside me this minute and rip me open. Or He could just stand on the floor of the everything—if such a thing is possible—and smash my head with His fist the size of this galaxy, or a million others. If He created me, He could just wipe me clean from existence, or turn me into a goat, sloth, or bunny. These thoughts hurt my mind, invisible next to His, and considering how puny mine is next to others I knew in life, those who ran companies and coded websites and edited magazines, I know I cannot hope to spar with the maker of all that has been or will be. My only hope is that I will find God in a vulnerable state, in a moment of mourning as He looks back at how He once killed everything He ever created in a flood, or sad He bet with the devil over a man's life, or asked a man to take his son to a mountain for sacrifice only to stop him at the last second. He could even be lamenting the creation of Judas, who God must have known from the start would betray Him. Or, worst of all, He could be depressed about torturing His own son, when all it would've taken to save us was better planning. I can bring up all those things, but I know as I go farther and farther, or maybe closer and closer, I will be afraid to meet Him. I am afraid of the one who is supposed to love me more than anyone else.

Once I read His words and believed, but later dismissed them, not wanting to try and weave together all their disparate threads. That's a liar's way of saying it. More so, I did not want to feel guilty. I understand there are those who are able to do both, love God and not feel guilty, and they would say, like Paul, "all things in moderation," or as those in the modern church say, "don't take everything so literally," but I could never root out where the literal stopped and the metaphorical began. So I left it behind, and my family prayed for me to regain it, but it was gone, and while not having it seemed to make my life better for a while, not having faith cannot, as I learned, take away a disposition to failure.

I call out in space, but He does not answer. Just more empty silence, which I liked at first but now seems ominous. I try not to think, hoping that might bring Him out of hiding. Plenty of times on earth I thought about God, though it never made Him appear. Some have claimed that works, I know. It's just that those people never seemed like very reliable sources. I start to recite the scriptures I remember, but as I begin I realize I never memorized many verses.

"For God so loved the World He gave his only son that whosoever shall believe in Him will not die but have eternal life. For God so loved the World He gave His only son that whosoever shall believe in Him will not die but have eternal life."

I never learned more? One of the epistles? A psalm? I start over, "For God so loved the World He…" And that's when it happens. God is here. I see Him.

Seeing God might be the wrong way to say it. I don't think anyone ever "sees" God. But he's here, just the same. He does not look like anyone in particular. Maybe like me, but much bigger, with a halo of globes and stars and asteroids, and if that's supposed to intimidate me, I don't know. It just makes me feel bad. Even though He created everything that ever was, He still has to put on a show. He hear me thinking that because just as soon the planets and stars disband and go back to their places. Now He is floating in front of me, in my human form: the same tired eyes, thick, useless calves, and red beard. He is naked, though, with a very large penis. The biggest one I have ever seen. As God, I would do the same thing.

"What are you doing?" He asks.

I think about the question, then about God thinking about me thinking about it. That sort of self-analysis is not doing either of us any good, so I try to answer Him as best as I can, even if He knows what I am going to say.

"I'm not even sure how this whole thing got started. If I'm alive or dead. I thought at first this was a way for me to get answers, but then that started to feel superficial, like something I'd seen in a movie?" As I speak, God listens as well as anyone ever has, though anything less than that would be a disappointment. I continue. "I also thought maybe I was being punished for the things I'd done. For the thoughts I've had and ways I've treated people? But then I thought maybe I was being punished for trying to rationalize my goodness, that no matter how well I think I treated people, I was always too easy on myself, and we all deserve punishment."

God nods, as if I am proving His point.

"You know why I'm here, don't You? I want to know, did You write my story at the beginning before anything else You ever created? And do You do that for everyone? Do You write their lives, how'll they go, before they were born? You knew every one of my steps before there were stars, or is it something I did after that made my story? Did I make myself bald? Did I do something that kept me from a job that would make me liked on social media? Was there some kind of step I took that forever steered me away from success? Did You write for me a grandness but somehow I mucked it up? What if I did something with my story that made it sour? It seems like the way things were set up I should have had a good story, but does everyone feel that way? Does everyone think their story is going to be great but somewhere along the way it goes wrong and they never know why?"

I have asked the question as best as I can ask it, and I am exhausted. I feel like I could sleep forever and that would be just enough.

"Before I answer," God says, "do you want to know?"

"I do," I say immediately, which I think surprises Him, my confident alacrity.

"It's both." God says. "I did write your story and you did undo it."

I am resigned, more than anything else, but I am also confused, so I ask, "I didn't know my story before I existed, so how could I have screwed it up? I lived the best way I could and that was the story I wrote. Right?"

"Yes, but you see, Jeffrey, because I am infinite, I did write your story before anything and at the same time you did undo it, because you lived in your terrestrial world in your mortal form where time did exist."

"But I couldn't understand that, God, like You just said, I was a human, wearing my bones and water and meat and blood. How was I supposed to know what my story was and if I was messing it up?"

God then stutters. He starts a sentence then stops, and everything around us—moons orbiting planets, space particles whizzing by, time—halts with the force it was once set forward upon. And now I am alone in the universe. Here I am devoid of color or mass or structure, and for a second I feel bad. God was trying to give me the best answer He could. With the way everything went with those He made, He had to send Himself to die to fix it, but even that couldn't mend the wound.

I like to think our conversation is what caused Him to give up and disappear to wherever it is the old gods go. But I am sure He had to be tired and used it as an excuse. Infinity is a long time to try.

—◦◦◦◦—

Alone with nothing, and this nothing, I think, has a lot of promise. I am rejuvenated by it. Like the old me who thought a new love waited, or a writing opportunity, or later still a job that would pay a respectable amount of money. Back then I believed that if I just kept getting up and trying, I'd get there. I was sure I had been built for a good life with a perfect partner and almost no worries. It was that part of me who decided to start over.

With what happened in the last world, I knew a danger lied in doing what I wanted to do, but I really did feel, as I began to form the first worlds, that I could do better. I made a promise with myself to not make things that look like Me, and if that did accidentally happen, if those types did start popping up, I would never be so conceited to make them worship Me all day every day. They would not be going anywhere when they died and I wanted them to know that. I wanted them to be happy. I wanted them to be good to one another.

A long time goes by, and what I made lives inside of Me. All of it is good, as I used only the parts of My imagination containing good things. Granted, My creation is not as impressive as the last. I do not have the mathematical skills nor the scientific reasoning to construct such wonders. Still I like to think My creations do less bickering and there are fewer terrible things done to each other in My Name. I never drown anyone or put anyone in a den of lions to prove My existence and no one blows themselves up to get closer to Me. For a long time, I am glad knowing that almost none of my creatures believe I exist at all.

Then one day I notice one of the creatures looking up at Me. This creature was a troubled one from the start. For whatever reason, he could never be happy with the lot I gave him. He always thought something better should happen, always feeling like he'd done something wrong. I need to save him. So I take My hand down into their world and pick him up. And yes he is screaming right before I squeeze him. But the noise is so tiny, it barely makes a squeak.

A HISTORY OF ALMOST EVERYTHING

There is a picture of my mother holding me on the morning of my birth in the middle of summer. They say it was the hottest day that year.

Later, my first word is "ball." I was chubby with blonde hair. My older sisters dressed me up in leotards so I could be a part of their home dance recitals.

I grew up on a farm, but I was not a farm boy. The most I did was pick strawberries. Sometimes I fed the sheep clover. I was once taken to see the baby chicks. They moved like a blanket of fluff and sounded like a million yellow phones all getting text alerts at once.

We had puppies and I had an imaginary friend named Johnny. We set a place for him at the table. On Sunday evenings we watched

Disney movies and my parents drove us miles on gravel roads to go trick-or-treating. We had a Slip'N Slide, and I went to church and Sunday school. My mom pulled me and my sisters in a red wagon to the end of driveway to get the mail.

We moved to town when I was seven. Cattle grazed beyond our fence in the backyard. I made friends with the boys down the block. Dale, whose dad was a highway patrolman, and Bob, whose dad was the principal at the public school. We played basketball in his driveway *Tecmo Bowl* in basements. Bob used the 49ers and I used the Bills. Ronnie Lott was so fast, I always lost. Down the street was my elementary school, and because I didn't smell I made friends.

In the summer I played Little League and rode my bike and swam at the pool. I played catch with my dad. He had cows in the country and I held down the calves when he cut off their testicles in the spring. When I got older, they called me E.T. because of my oblong head. In the fourth grade I got my first mechanical pencil and pushed the lead into my palm to see how far it would go. The spot it left remains. On weekends I was driven to my best friend's house in the country. In town, my middle sister and I constructed tree fort named after a John Denver song. I once threw my oldest sister's *Chicago* tape against our brick fireplace. Neither of us can remember why.

In my room on the wooden dresser with the mirror there were three figurines—Larry Bird, Magic Johnson, Michael Jordan—even though I wanted to be a professional baseball player. I could not understand math and speech therapy was once a week. When I was twelve my dad drove us, my sisters and my mom—a teacher—six blocks to the "big building." On my first day of junior high I did the Fresh Prince high step. A high school wrestler imitated my move for the study hall, and I suddenly understood adolescence.

I came off the bench in sports, starting once at basketball, but was quickly winded. I have betathalassemia minor, I told everyone, "if it was the major case I'd die." I sang in the choirs, at school and church, and as I got older played football, but my head was too big for any regular helmet. My junior year I gave Maggie a zerbert. Her brother was the biggest on our football team. He lifted weights at the age of twelve and was the son of a milk farmer. The day after I did it—the night before we'd been playing Truth or Dare at Bob's house—I came in for first-period choir and Marvin, who gave me wedgies, and Aaron, who gave Tim the impossible sit-up, and Cody, who always asked if I filmed my sister naked and masturbated to the films, were making loud slobbering noises. It was because of the zerbert, but more than that, it was an allusion to my lisp from years before.

My senior year, my best friend drifted to drugs and I drifted to God. I became friends with the kids from Mennonite school. I wore Beck t-shirts and periwinkle pants and dated a girl from the private school. We watched *The Shawshank Redemption* one summer night and I kissed her nipples. We broke up after she wrote a note and Kim, our friend, delivered it. It was the first time I heard the phrase "we're better off as friends." I went to prom with another girl from the private school and qualified for state in golf. Trips to Sioux Falls for movies with Evan and Paul. Things were easy.

I attended a land-grant university two hours from where I was born. My second semester I drank a beer for the first time and the same night found myself in a lofted bed with a woman. We did things I had always wanted to do. But she was pregnant, I just knew it, even though we had not had sex. So I prayed and since there was no baby I devoted myself to God. I didn't kiss another for six years. I wrote for the student newspaper and was the music director at the college radio station. I wanted to write but didn't change my major, "because it didn't matter, God could use me anywhere."

One summer in college to Colorado where I proselytized to strangers. The next summer, the fall before I student-taught and graduated, I interned at a Christian music magazine in Texas. I looked at naked women on the internet and believed God punished me by making me go bald each time I did.

I worked as an in-school suspension supervisor after college and wrote for *Pitchfork* as a newswriter. I moved to Nebraska where I worked at a group home and fell in love with a houseparent. I worked there for a year and for the year after that I thought about the houseparent while working at a group home in Sioux Falls at night and at a package delivery company by day. I played video games in my spare time. Everyone was married or getting married and that's when I met the second. She was from Alabama and we found each other on MySpace. I visited her in the South and we did more than I had ever done without clothes. When I got back to my place in Sioux Falls she texted to say I was not the spiritual leader she was looking for. I went to my sister's house, and as I hugged her I cried longer than I thought I could. I met my first hipsters in Sioux Falls, but I needed to be free from the ones having children and the ones doing mushrooms in pastures. My editor from Texas lived in Seattle and was no longer a Christian, and as I drove to Spokane, Washington from Sioux Falls, South Dakota in one day I listened to a book on tape and decided I wasn't either. Before I left, though, I was with someone. She worked at the group home and was half-black half-white and had the most amazing backside I had seen or ever will, I imagine.

In Seattle I met housebuilders and volunteers and people who grew backyard gardens. They whittled wood and drank wine and played Frisbee and kickball. I also met the one with curly hair, and other women, and they were interested in me as more than friends. I wandered into their beds and they wandered into mine, and by the fall of that year the one with curly hair had had enough. She moved away for school and I told myself I didn't care. I started writing again. I wanted to write a novel to take down Joshua Harris. My *Blankets*. After a year I submitted it to agents and small presses and received two letters of interest, one from a vanity press. I worked at the same package delivery company and hoped to be promoted as my housebuilder friends began to pair up and move to the suburbs. I missed the one with curly hair.

I got fatter and balder. I gave away my car. I moved closer to home. In Minneapolis I lived in the attic of my friend's house. The day I arrived he was eating a fifty-piece Chicken McNugget meal. I joined a gym y and bought a car. It drove me to a temp job I hated more than any job I'd had in my life. With my itinerant life, I had no connections for a career. I studied for the GRE but started a blog instead of taking the test. I online dated and met a good person who I broke up with twice, once in person and once over email.

I quit the temp job where I watched bottles of medicine go by alongside immigrants from Laos and Somalia and started working at *Barnes & Noble* in the shipping department, and I online dated. Over the next years I saw maybe one hundred or so people. One of them was a dark-haired Jewish woman from the East Coast who had just graduated from Carleton. I wrote a story about how things went with us and I sent it to her, then she deleted her profile and reinstated it a week later. It went like that a number of times with a number of other people.

I began to submit my writing again. Not to agents but to local blogs. I was told by an editor, after his fifth or sixth rejected submission, to submit to *Thought Catalog*. So I did, and after several rejected submissions I started writing for them but did not get paid. I quit my job at *Barnes & Noble* and wrote without a day job for the first time in my life. I submitted short stories to journals. After all rejections, I started working at a steel factory. I stopped writing and began to think being published was for other people. I stopped online dating. I went to a wedding in Charleston and met someone. I quit my job at the steel factory and moved in with her.

In Milwaukee I start writing again. I find I have amassed hundreds of blog posts, thirty short stories, two novellas, and three novels. I begin to submit my stories again. I join another gym, this time an organized class. The psychiatrist and I talk of marriage.

ACKNOWLEDGEMENTS

Thank you, Phil. Your support has meant a lot. Thank you as well to Kristin for the fine editing, and to Liz for the wonderful covers. Thank you, Mom and Dad. Not sure when you'll ever read this, but thank you for everything just the same. And thank you once more to my wife. Once more is not enough, but I don't know how long it would take to print the same words infinitely: Thank you. I love you.